William B. Lane

Life of our President Benjamin Harrison

Together With That of His Grandfather William Henry Harrison

William B. Lane

Life of our President Benjamin Harrison
Together With That of His Grandfather William Henry Harrison

ISBN/EAN: 9783743410114

Manufactured in Europe, USA, Canada, Australia, Japa

Cover: Foto ©Raphael Reischuk / pixelio.de

Manufactured and distributed by brebook publishing software
(www.brebook.com)

William B. Lane

Life of our President Benjamin Harrison

FIRST EDITION.   TWENTY-FIVE CENTS.

LIFE OF

GRANDFATH. .?

AND GRANDSON.

LIFE

OF

Our President

Benjamin Harrison,

TOGETHER WITH THAT OF

His Grandfather

WILLIAM HENRY HARRISON

The "Hero of Tippecanoe" and President 1841.

Printed by
THE ECONONY PRINTING CO., 304 VINE ST., CINCINNATI
For LANE & MORRISON. Publishers,
1889.

PREFACE.

To the CITIZENS *and* PATRIOTS *of the United States this work is respectfully dedicated.*

The subject is a noble one. Whether in the present instance justice has been done to it or not, you must decide. It tells of a hero. Not of one like Napoleon. or Cæsar, or Alexander—those proud oppressors of mankind, who rose and flourished at the expense of the happiness of millions—but of a *republican* hero—plain, unostentatious, and benevolent—of a *patriot* whose delight has been to serve his country, and contribute to the protection and comfort of the defenceless inhabitants of our frontier. It tells of one. who, forsaking the scenes of his youth and the pleasures of society, went forth into our western wilds and amid toils, privations, and sufferings, raised himself to honor and influence by his own personal efforts. He entered the army. He fought with savages. He drove them from the unprotected and defenceless habitation of the widow. He established peace; and now where comparatively only a few years since the war-whoop carried consternation, there are fellow-citizens dwelling in safety;

and where once were the habitations of cruelty, are seen the temples of the Living God.

It tells us of a hero, who, having achieved the security and independence of the West, returned, like Washington at an earlier day, to private life, to the cultivation of a farm, to the quiet and unostentatious residence of a LOG CABIN more honorable than the gorgeous palaces of the eastern world.

Such men are an honor to our country. We have had many such, to whom the people of the United States could "look up to in time of danger," who guided our councils, who led our armies, who achieved our independence.

But they are nearly all gone. A few noble stocks remain. Let us do them honor. Let us show them gratitude. Let us employ their wisdom and experience in times of difficulty and trial.

Therefore, from what better stock could we choose a captain to stand at the helm of State and steer our glorious party through the intricate channels of statesmanship? and in electing Benj. Harrison (grandson of this grand old hero) as President we have every confidence that such an one has been choosen to fill the position.

Added to the life of his grandfather, we have appended a brief review of his career up the present time; and in bringing this work before the public, we trust that any shortcomings will be over-looked.

Therefore with sincere and heartfelt wishes that the future may bring a term of prosperity to the country at large under his administration, such as we have never before experienced, we submit this work to your kin dindulgence, and respectfully make our bow.

Remaining your well-wishers,

THE AUTHORS.

CONTENTS.

THE HERO OF TIPPECANOE.

Jose Earle hears of the General in a grocery store.

CHAPTER I.

Wherein Jose Earle meets with an adventure which lays the foundation of the present volume.

"The Hero of Tippecanoe!"—"The Hero of Tippecanoe!" The words rang in the ears of little Jose Earle, as he returned towards home from a grocery, where he had been to purchase a few pounds of sugar for his mother. "I wonder who this Hero of Tippecanoe can be?"

While standing at the counter, waiting for tne clerk to put up the article he wished, his attention has been drawn to a somewhat spirited, but by no means angry, conversation between several men of the village, as to the merits of this said "Hero." He was not present when the conversation was begun.   One said he was a good soldier; another that he was a famous general; and so they went round, talking of the battles he had fought—of the Indians he had taken; and, finally, some half-dozen declared, that they almost knew he would be *President of the United States.*

"I'll venture a mug of ale on that;" said a surly looking man, stepping forward, and addressing himself to one of the individuals in the circle.

"I never bet," said the man; "it is against my principles; but if I were going to bet, it wouldn't be *ale*, but a little *'hard cider,'*"—with a peculiar emphasis on the two last words; "but I don't bet."

"Well, well," said the man, "let that pass, but he won't be president, this year, nor next—"

"I didn't know about *next* year; but I rather *guess* on the 4th of March, 1841, his LOG CABIN will be exchanged for the WHITE HOUSE."

"Never — never," said the man, with some warmth; "he'll never see the inside of that house, unless he dines with Martin Van Buren."

"So you think?"

"Yes, so I think—so I—"

He was going to say, "so I *know;*" but, like a wise man, he checked himself and said, "*believe.*"

Jose was an attentive listener to the conversation, during which he had tried hard to learn who this "Hero of Tippecanoe" was. He knew that it did not mean Mr. Van Buren. He never heard *him* called a hero; and he concluded they did not mean General Jackson, for he was called the "Hero of New Orleans." Whom did they mean? That was more than he could tell. The name sounded musical, and even heroic, and he waited quite impatiently to learn who the hero was.

But something whispered, or seemed to whisper, in Jose's ear, that he must not stay any longer, even to gratify a laudable curiosity. His mother had taught him—and certainly it is a good lesson for all boys to learn and practice—to do an errand, and return as quickly as possibe.

Accordingly, although the conversation was still going on, Jose retreated towards the door, but rather slowly; and even when his fingers were on the latch, he was half inclined to step back, and ask a man in the circle whom he knew, about whom they were talking; but a commendable modesty kept him back. His curiosity, however, had been too much excited to remain long quiet; and, determining to gratify it in another place, he opened the door, and directed his step homeward.

Jose, my readers must know was quite young; and, while most lads of his age might, perhaps, have answered the question, it was out of his power. And a good reason existed for his ignorance. He had recently returned home, from having lived with a maiden aunt, where the subject of politics was as little likely to be discussed, as who would be the next king of England or France. Jose was not aware that a new presidential election was drawing near, nor that the conversation to which he had listened was turning upon the merits of the several candidates for that office before the public. But Jose had a good memory, from which a name so charming to his ear was not likely to escape, or if there was any real danger in the case, his frequent repetition of it, as he sauntered along, was sufficient to keep it alive. Indeed, had there been any passers-by, it is quite probable they would have heard him humming a kind of tune: "The Hero—the Hero—the Hero of Tip—the Hero of Tippecanoe! Tippecanoe!"

Soon after turning a corner in sight of his father's, he descried at some distance before him a school-fellow by the name of Jimmy Goodspeed.

"Jimmy—Jimmy—Jimmy Goodspeed!" holloed Jose, "stop!"

"What do you want, Jose?"

"Wait, and I'll tell you."

"Well, make haste. If your legs were as long

again, you'd walk a little faster when a fellow is
waiting for you."

"I'm almost out of breath now," said Jose, as he
came up, his face glowing with animation.

"Well, what's your wish, Jose? shall I help you
carry your bundle?"

"Oh, no," said Jose, "I can carry that. What I
want is, to know whether you ever heard of—*there*,
now, you've almost made me forget what I was going to say. Have you ever heard of—of—oh, I
know now of 'The Hero of Tippecanoe?'"

"Heard of him? ha, ha, ha? Why, child, more
times than you ever eat supper in all your life. But
he's no great things."

"But who is he?" said Jose, "that was my question. They don't mean General Jackson, do they?"

"Take care, Jose, my friend. Jose, take care how
you talk about General Jackson. I'm a true Jackson man, do you know that?"

"I didn't mean any harm, Jimmy; but I heard
some men up at Peter Crowfoot's store talking rather loud and fast about the 'Hero of Tippecanoe,'
and I thought you could tell me."

"Well, I suppose I could, but I don't want to talk
about him; besides, you are to young to talk politics, Jose."

The lads here separated, Jose having arrived at
his father's. Jimmy had still further to go, and bid-
ding his little friend good-morning, said:

" 'Log cabin and hard cider' won't be president this year or next, mark my word, Joe."

Jose tried to laugh, but as he didn't understand what was meant, he made a poor figure of it; but as the gate swung to, he said "Well, Jimmy, you'll not find me so ignorant next time we meet. Father, I guess, knows all about the matter."

Jimmy plodded on. He was the son of a true Jacksonian, and of course felt and talked just as his father did. He tried to believe that Mr. Van Buren would be elected president again, because his father tried to believe so; but he had heard his father say there began to be some doubt. Strange alterations were taking place. Matters didn't work well. The times were hard. Jimmy's father didn't get as much work as he had done; and when he did, not much more than half as much in price, and very little money. Jimmy fell into quite a serious train of reflection after leaving Jose; and, I believe, before he reached the place to which he was going, a couplet, which he had either seen, or himself manufactured, was occupying his thoughts. I do not know that he sung it, but quite likely he did; for who did not begin to sing something like it?

> Tippy, old Tippy, I very much fear,
> You'll take the *Great Chair* the very next year.

Captain Earle conversing with his family.

CHAPTER II.

Some explanations; in making which, certain new actors appear on the stage. Jose learns who the "Hero of Tippicanoe" is.

IT is quite time to introduce our readers to the family of Captain Earle, the father of our friend Jose. But a few words will suffice to give such details of his history, as are important to our purpose.

Captain Earle I shall suppose to have been an officer of the army, during a considerable part of Mr. Madison's war. He served with great reputa-

tion, was in several battles at the West, and was
most enthusiastically attached, as most of the officers
of the northwestern army were, to their brave commander, GENERAL WILLIAM HENRY HARRISON.

At the close of the war, he returned to his native
state; and after living some years a bachelor, married the daughter of a military officer, who was con-
siderably his senior in the army, and settled in the
village of——.

He had several sons. His eldest he named *William Henry Harrison*, after his admired general,
with whom he had an intimate and honorable ac-
quaintance. In respect to the name of his second
son, we must premise an explanation. Being himself a military man, it was natural that, like most of
the military men of the country, he should have been
attached to the cause of General Jackson. As a
military hero, there was much to admire in the general's character. But he was thought by some to be
arbitrary, and in some cases cruel. Still, he was
bold and successful. At New Orleans, he had
achieved a victory which established his reputation.
Captain Earle was among the number who thought
that he would shine in the cabinet as he had done in
the field; and, besides, in common with others, he
felt a sort of gratitude to a man, who had long per-
illed his life and happiness among savages for his
country. He supported him, therefore, for the presi-

dency, and, like a good many others, on the birth of his second son, he named him *Andrew Jackson*, after the general, who had at the time just entered upon his office as president.   His third son bore the name of *Thomas;* and his fourth and last, the hero of the adventure related in the first chapter, *Joseph* or, as he was more commonly called, *Jose*.   The two latter were family names; the one, that of an only brother of the captain, and the other, that of a brother of his wife.   Mrs. Earle was a woman of strong good sense, quite domestic, but not unconcerned in all that interested her husband and his fortunes; and, being the daughter of a patriot, she had early learned to love and desire the welfare of her country.

But Captain Earle, like thousands of others, was deceived in the ability of General Jackson to wield successfully the destinies of America.   He knew his reputation as a military man, and he fondly imagined that he would be equally successful as president of the United States; but he was sadly disappointed. He watched the progress of his administration, and was grieved to find that within a few years the country, which was so prosperous, became so embarrassed and disturbed.   But, like others, he had enlisted himself—it was known that he was one of the Jackson party—he had talked, written, and acted for and with that party.   When, in 1837, General Jackson intimated his intention to retire, and General

Harrison was brought out as a candidate, Captain Earle had quite a struggle in his own feelings what to do. He preferred his old friend, General Harrisson, but then he belonged to the Jackson party, and his circumstances did not then seem to admit of his enlisting even for an old friend. So he voted for Mr. Van Buren. But he soon saw his error, and most heartily repented. Mr. Van Buren's measures, he became satisfied, were still worse than those of General Jackson.

The change which thus came over Captain Earle he was not slow to avow; and as the time approached for the election of a new president, Captain Earle would say, "I can go no longer for Mr. Van Buren, nor for any administration whose principles and measures are like his."

I have heard him sit down and talk after this manner:

"If I had a ship which always made long and unprofitable voyages, which brought me in debt, instead of adding to my gains, I should be quite likely to inquire into the matter. Why does this ship do so poorly, when others do so well in the same trade? Is she a bad ship? are her sails poor? is her rudder too small? or what is the mattter? Perhaps her *captain* is in fault. But he had a high reputation when I first employed him. Almost every one said he would do well—he made fair promises—and really appeared to be honest and well-meaning. But then *the ship dosen't work well.* And yet she was projected and built by the very first mechanics, and has been examined by them repeatedly, and they say the reason why she makes poor voyages is not that the ship is in fault; she has made good voyages, and would make them again, if she had a *more competent captain.*

"Now," said Captain Earle, "in such a case, what should I be likely to do? Why, notwithstanding the *reputation* of my captain, I should be quite likely to *change* him for another. I might think him *honest* and *well-disposed;* but still I should say, I can not afford to *lose* every thing to *gratify him,* or keep him in a *good berth. I will try another captain, and see whether the old ship won't do better.*"

So Captain Earle reasons; and not a few of his neighbors, who value his opinions because they think him a wise and good man, have adopted them, and say the ship must have a new captain. The right ropes are not pulled. The right course is not pursued. One voyage under General Jackson proved a bad one, and so has that under Mr. Van Buren. Even if they are honest and well-disposed, they are not capable. The ship goes wrong. We must try another captain.

At the time our friend Jose arrived from the grocery, the tea was ready and waiting. Captain Earle, who was reading a newspaper which had just arrived, though deeply interested in the views it contained, laid it aside, and the family were soon engaged in taking their tea.

Jose was in his usual place, and for once seemed to be quite absorbed in his own thoughts, until Captain Earle remarked to his wife that really the "old Hero's" prospects of success were brightening every day.

At the mention of the "old hero," Jose seemed to wake up as from a dream. "Father," said he, "I heard some men up at the store talking about the 'Hero of Tippecanoe.' Pray, who is he? I never heard of such a hero."

"Why, my son, never heard of your father's old general! but you are a small boy. You have heard of the 'Here of New Orleans?'"

"Yes, sir," said Jose; "brother Andrew was named after him, but I don't think Andrew much of a hero."

"Your opinion, Jose, settles that point, I suppose you think," said Andrew; "but I shall stick to the 'Hero of New Orleans,' a little longer, I believe."

"I should think you would like to change your name," said Thomas, "so much is said against General Jackson now-a-days."

"No—not I, I wish I were half as brave as the old general is."

"Names are but of small importance, my children," said Mrs. Earle; "it is far more important to be wise and good."

"But, father," said Jose, who had stopped eating, "you've not told me who the 'Hero of Tippecanoe' is. I asked Jimmy Goodspeed, but—"

"Well, and what did Jimmy say?"

"Why, he said he new, but he did not like to talk about him."

Captain Earle smiled. "There are many," said he, "who feel very much as Jimmy does. They do not like to read, hear, or talk about him. But you wish to know who he is; let me introduce you to him across the table, *Master William Henry Harrison.*"

"William! What, William, are you the 'Hero of Tippecanoe?'" said Jose.

"Don't you think I am? don't I look like a hero?"

"You would look, I think, a little more like one," said Jose, if you sat up a little straighter."

"Why, Jose, you seem to be quite sharp this evening," said William. "I'll try to be a hero, then. There! what do you say now?"

"I am glad master Jose has such a correct idea of a hero," said Mrs. Earle; "*straight* in body; but it is equally essential to the *true* hero, that he should be *straight* or *upright*, in mind."

"Well, let us now answer Jose's inquiry," said

Captain Earle. "The 'Hero of Tippecanoe' is *William Henry Harrison*, a famous general, who lives in Ohio, and who commanded the northwestern army during the late war with England."

"Was William named after him?" said Jose.

"Yes, my son. I served under General Harrison during a considerable part of the war. He is a good man. I knew him well, and I wish all the American people knew him as well as I do. There would then be little doubt of his election."

"Some men up at the store," interrupted Jose, "said he is going to be president; but one man, who appeared almost angry, declared he never would be."

"He meant, he hoped he wouldn't be. There are many who hope so, but more, I suspect, who hope he will be. A great change is taking place. I read a fine song this evening in the paper, entitled 'Old Tip.' Here it is. 'The last verse runs thus:

'The people are coming, from plain and from mountain,
  To join the brave band of the honest and free,
Which grows, as the stream from the leaf-sheltered fountain,
  Spreads broad and more broad till it reaches the sea;
No strength can restrain it, no force can retain it,
  Whate'er may resist, it breaks gallantly through,
And borne by its motion as a ship on the ocean,
  Speeds on in his glory old Tippecanoe,
    The iron-hearted soldier, the true-hearted soldier,
    The gallant old soldier of Tippecanoe.'

"They are 'coming'—'the people'—the 'people from plain and from mountain," said Captain Earle, "There is no stopping the progress of this enthusiasm. It rolls on, and, for aught I know, it will roll. General Harrison will, I think, take possession of the ' *White House*' March 4, 1841."

"You will be the first to go and congratulate him, I conclude," said Andrew, rather significantly, "you like him so much, father."

"I do like him, my son," replied Captain Earle, "and I have great reason for my regard."

"You *once* thought highly of *Andrew Jackson*."

"*Andrew Jackson Earle* I love now, and trust I shall ever have reason to love him. I did once regard *General Andrew Jackson* with much favor, but as president of the United States he has disappointed me."

"Father, when you go to see President Harrison, may I go too?" inquired Jose.

"It will be time enough to decide that question when he is elected."

"But you said, you believe he will be elected."

"I do, my son, I hope he will, I believe he will. He is an able and a good man, and has done much for his country. He deserves well of it."

"Father," said Thomas, "I was just going to ask you to tell us something about his life. You must know a good deal about him."

"So do, said Jose ; "I love to hear stories."

"There are many interesting incidents in the life of General Harrison," said Captain Earle. "It will give me pleasure to relate them. After the table is removed, and I have written a letter, I will at least make a beginning."

Young Harrison reading the commission of ensign from Gen. Washington.

CHAPTER III.

Conversation at Captain Earle's about the "Hero of Tippecanoe," during which the Captain talks more than all the rest.

WE left Captain Earle and his family still at the tea-table, making arrangements for spending the evening in reciting and listening to some recollections of the "old Hero!" Which of the group was the more pleased with the proposal, the father or the sons, I cannot undertake to say; but there was more than ordinary despatch that evening in writing the letter to which the former alluded at the table as necessary to be done; and nearly as soon as Mrs. Earle had adjusted the sitting room for the evening, the several parties made their appearance. A table was occupying the centre of the room, around which they took their seats, and on which Captain Earle laid several papers, which he said he might need by way of illustration in the progress of his remarks.

"This is a happy hour," said the captain, as he drew a chair to the table. "I love to know that my sons are fond of hearing about the history of their country, and of the men who have fought her battles, and have figured in her councils. We have had many great men—noble men—patriots, who sacrificed ease, health, fortune, and life for their country. But they have passed away. All who braved the storms of the revolution are already gone. But

> Theirs is no vulgar sepulchre; green sods
> Are all their monument—and yet it tells
> A nobler history than pillar'd pile,
> Or the eternal pyramid. They need
> No statue, nor inscription to reveal
> Their greatness.

"I delight to converse with them, even if they are gone, or going—to dwell upon their exalted patriotism—their firmness in the day of peril—their adherence to principle, at the hazard of their lives—

their faith and steadfastness, when shipwreck and ruin stared them in the face—their fortitude under privation and suffering—their magnanimity and sympathy in the day of victory and triumph. I hope, my sons, you will read their history, and I am sure you will venerate and love them. Imitate their virtues, their patriotism, their piety, and I shall feel proud of my sons."

"Father," said Jose, "I thought you were going to tell about General Harrison—"

"Don't be so fast, Jose," said William; "I'm sure I should like to hear father talk thus all night."

"You do me great honor, my son," said Captain Earle. "On such a theme I scarcely know when to stop. But it is time, I believe, to gratify Jose.

"William Henry Harrison is a native of Virginia. His birthplace is Berkley, a town or village situated on the banks of James River, about twenty-five miles below Richmond, and forty miles above Jamestown.

"At this place William Henry Harrison was born, February 9th, 1773."

"He is quite an old man," said Andrew, "as old, I guess, as my namesake; and no one would think of so old a man for president as General Jackson is now."

"You mistake, my son," said Captain Earle. "General Jackson was born on the 15th of March, 1767. Hence he is six years older than General Harrison.

"William Henry was the third and youngest son of BENJAMIN HARRISON, who was a distinguished man in Virginia, and a member of the celebrated congress of 1774 and 1776."

"My history of the United States says he was one who *signed the Declaration of Independence*," said Thomas.

"I am glad you so well recollect your history," said Captain Earle. "That was a noble body of men, and as long as America lasts, their boldness in signing and publishing that Declaration will be remembered with patriotism."

"Father," observed William, "you speak of *boldness*, I don't see what great courage was needed."

"It is because of your ignorance, my son. The Declaration of Independence was one of the boldest acts of the revolution. Napoleon never took a bolder step. There were thirteen colonies; but they were feeble, with less than three millions of people, no veteran army, no navy, no arsenals but barns, no munitions of war, scarcely a fortification, no public treasury, no power to lay a tax, and no credit upon which to obtain a loan.

"Was there nothing bold in such a people rising up against England, and saying they were **free**, and would be free and independent? England was the mistress of the world; her armies were numerous, her soldiers veterans, her navy unrivalled, her

statesmen subtle and sagacious, her generals skilful
and practised.

"All this the congress of '76 well knew. And
they knew that if they published that Declaration,
and any one of them should be taken by the English, he would be hung. And this was quite likely
to come to pass. It was a solemn time therefore
with them, and a solemn question, whether they
should make such a declaration.

"But the question went round. 'Shall the Declaration be adopted?' Each rose and said ' *Yes*.'
William Henry Harrison's father was there, and he
said ' *Yes*.' The whole fifty-six said 'Yes'—not a
solitary '*Nay*.' It was a great occasion. In due
time, after the question was taken, the Declaration
was written neatly and fairly on parchment, which
was brought in to be signed by the several members.

"*John Hancock* being president, signed his name
first. It is remakable how strong he bore down
upon his pen. It seemed as if he meant to say, 'If
this be an act of treason, it shall be treason indeed.'
Each one followed him, each wrote his name with
the same pen, and that pen is still preserved.

"Benjamin Harrison, the father of William Henry,
was among the number; and there his name will
stand, and the names of his patriotic associates, as
long as America lasts, a noble monument of their
courage, patriotism and *fidelity*.

"I don't mean to intimate, my children," continued Captain Earle, "that any one has a claim to office *because his ancestors were great and honorable*, or because they performed eminent service to their country. But a virtuous, high-minded, and useful ancestry, is always regarded as honorable. We are so made as to put this estimate upon it; and he that is so fortunate as to have such ancestors, should feel his responsibility to imitate their virtues. It is a powerful motive to pattern after them; and the instances are not few in the country, where sons, much to their honor, have followed in the footsteps of their illustrious sires. William Henry Harrison is a fine example.

"I shall only add in respect to his father, that he afterwards held several distinguished offices in Virginia, and among them that of governor. At length he died, 1791, leaving behind him the reputation of a devoted patriot, an able counsellor, and a useful man."

"Many of the patriots of the revolution died comparatively poor. They had no opportunity to acquire wealth, as their time, talents, and services were devoted to a country too poor to remunerate them. The little fortunes which they had acquired, were expended for their families while they were busy in the councils, and not a few of them were obliged to advance funds to aid in carrying forward the measures which their wisdom and patriotism decided to be necessary. Governor Harrison was among the number. He left his children little more than his example, and the good-will of his contemporary patriots.

"William Henry was at this time in the college of Hampden Sidney, pursuing his studies, preparatory to the study of medicine. As he was under age when his father died, Robert Morris, another distinguished man, consented to act as his guardian.

"Just about this time the country became greatly alarmed, in consequence of the ravages of Indians of the northwestern frontier. These tribes embraced the Miamies, Hurons, Delawares, Chippewas, and several others. They were powerful and warlike. The country was thinly inhabited. Families were exposed to their deadly hostility; and, in not a few instances, women and children were suddenly assaulted, and either barbarously wounded or carried into a long and distressing captivity.

"In 1790, General Harmar was appointed to take the field against these Indians. His force was about fifteen hundred men; three hundred and twenty of whom were regular troops, the rest militia.

"On the 30th of September, General Harmar set forth with his troops from Fort Washington, a fort which stood on a spot near which the city of Cincinnati has since been built. His object was to bring the Indians to an engagement. or. if that could not be effected. to destroy their settlement on the waters of the Scioto and Wabash.

"General Harmar had been an officer in the revolutionary war. and great things were expected of him. He succeeded in destroying some villages. and considerable quantities of corn. which the Indians had laid in store for the winter. But on his return. having arrived within eight miles of Chillicothe. he halted. with a view of doing something more for his honor and that of his army.

"From this place he detached three hundred and sixty men. with orders to find the enemy and attack them. This they did. But the engagement was unfortunate for the Americans. A considerable number of Indians were killed. but not less than one hundred of the militia fell during the engagement. among whom were ten officers. The survivors hastily retreated. and having joined the main body, the whole returned to Fort Washington.

"The result of this expedition was severely felt and deeply deplored. General Harmar was removed. and Major-general Arthur St. Clair was appointed to succeed him.

"Washington. at that time being president. was anxious to do all in his power to protect the frontier. and congress having voted him large sums to carry on the war. he ordered General St. Clair to undertake an expedition, in which he was directed to destroy the Indian villages on the.Miami, and to expel the savages from the country.

"Troops were enlisted slowly, and not until September had St. Clair such a number as he deemed necessary to enter upon the campaign. On the 3rd of November, with fourteen hundred men, he encamped on a commanding ground about fifteen miles south of the Miami village. The militia took a position across a creek, in advance of the regular soldiers.

"The next morning, about half an hour before sunrise, a body of Indians suddenly attacked the militia, who immediately fled across the creek, and rushing in where the regular soldiers were encamped, threw them into confusion. The officers sprung forward, and endeavored to rally their men. The Indians pursued with savage yells. The battle became terrible. The American soldiers poured in their fire, and the cannon spread destruction on every side, the Indians pressing up to their very mouths.

"At length resort was had to the bayonet; and now, for a short time, the Indians fell back; but they rallied again. The gallant General Butler fell, mortally wounded. But I can not," said Captain Earle, "pursue further the details of this disastrous contest. The defeat of the Americans was signal,

and the destruction appalling. Thirty-eight com-
missioned officers were killed on the field, and five
hundred and ninety-three non-commissioned officers
and privates were slain or missing. Between two
and three hundred officers and privates were wounded, many of whom afterwards died.

"But it is time to return to our young friend,
William Henry Harrison. He was, as I said, at this
time a member of college. The Indian war at the
west was engaging the attention of the country.
The spirits of many were roused, and young Harrison
was among the number. He panted for the field—
he longed for an opportunity to distinguish himself;
and, at length, he determined to abandon the halls of
college, and seek his fortune in the wilds of the west.

"Robert Morris, his guardian, for a time opposed
his design; but Washington, who had been an intimate friend of his father's, encouraged his youthful
genius, and gave him a commission, as ensign, in the
First Regiment of United States Artillery, then sta-
tioned at Fort Washington, on the Ohio.

"Ensign Harrison, yet only eighteen years of age,
soon departed for the scene of his toils. He was
young, ardent, and ambitious. He reached Fort
Washington shortly after St. Clair's defeat, and there
entered upon that line of services which for a period
of nearly forty years he continued; in all which he
sustained a reputation most honorable to himself and
useful to his country.

"I do not design, my children," said Captain Earle, "to follow Harrison through the various incidents of his life. They are so many, and so various, and so connected and interwoven with the history of the country, that it would prove tedious to your youthful minds. I will give you, in one view, the outlines of his eventful life, and afterwards notice such particular incidents as may seem most striking and important."

Here taking a paper from the table, he read as follows:

"William H. Harrison was born in Virginia, on the 9th of February, 1773.

"In 1791, when nineteen years of age, he was appointed by Washington an ensign in our infant army.

"In 1792, he was promoted to the rank of lieutenant; and in 1793 he joined the legion under General Wayne, and in a few days thereafter was selected by him as one of his aids.

"On the 24th of August, 1794, he distinguished himself in the battle of the Miami, and elicited the most flattering written approbation of General Wayne.

"In 1795, he was made captain, and was placed in command of Fort Washington.

"In 1797, he was appointed, by President Adams, secretary of the Northwestern Territory, and *ex-officio*, lieutenant-governor .

"In 1798, he was chosen a delegate to congress.

"In 1801, he was appointed governor of Indiana; and in the same year, President Jefferson appointed him sole commissioner for treating with the Indians.

"In 1809, he was reappointed governor of Indiana by Madison.

"On the 6th of November, 1811, he gained the great battle of *Tippecanoe.*

"On the 11th of September, 1812, he was appointed by Madison commander-in-chief of the northwestern army.

"On the 28th of April, 1813, the siege of Fort Meigs commenced, lasted twelve days, and was terminated by the brilliant and successful sortie of General Harrison.

"On the 31st of July, 1813, the battle of Fort Stephenson occurred.

"On the 5th of October, 1813, he gained the splendid victory of the *Thames,* over the British and Indians under Proctor.

"In 1814, he was appointed by Madison one of the commissioners to treat with the Indians; and in the same year, with his colleagues, Governor Shelby and General Cass, concluded his celebrated treaty of Greenville.

"In 1815, he was again appointed such commissioner with General McArthur and Mr. Graham, and negotiated a treaty at Detroit.

"In 1816, he was elected a member of congress.

"In January, 1818, he introduced a resolution in honor of Kosciusko, and supported it in one of the most feeling, classical, and eloquent speeches ever made in the house of representatives.

"In 1819, he was elected a member of the Ohio senate.

"In 1824, he was elected senator in congress, and was appointed in 1825 chairman of the military committee in place of General Jackson, who had resigned.

"In 1827, he was appointed minister to Colombia, and in 1828 wrote his immortal letter to Bolivar, the deliverer of South America."

"We will here conclude our relations to-night," said Captain Earle, "and, if alive and well, will resume to-morrow evening."

Escort of the Packhorses.

CHAPTER IV.

Captain Earle continues his conversation, in which he tells about further troubles with the Indians, and a decisive victory over them.

AT an early hour on the evening following, Captain Earle and his family were again seated round the table. He had become deeply interested in the recollections of former events himself, and there was no lack of attention on the part of his youthful auditors.

"I told you last evening, my children, that I did not purpose a regular biography of the 'Hero of Tippecanoe,' only sketches of some of the most prominent incidents of his life. This will be sufficient for my purpose, and will be more interesting to you.

"He reached Fort Washington, as I stated, soon after the defeat of St. Clair's army. That defeat was unexpected, and produced great consternation through the country. The depredations of the savages became more furious and ferocious than ever; and tragical scenes were enacted in various places along the frontier, and even in some of the most populous sections of the country.

"I could relate many affecting incidents which occurred, but will content myself with one, which happened somewhere about this time, and which will serve to show the temper of the savages, and the boldness and intrepidity of the frontier inhabitants.

"A dwelling-house, I believe in some part of Kentucky, not far from the borders of the Ohio, was attacked by a party of Indians. The proprietor, Mr. Merrill, was alarmed by the barking of his dog. On going to the door, he received the fire of the assailants, which broke his right leg and arm. They attempted to enter the house, but were anticipated in their movement by Mrs. Merrill and her daughter, who closed the door in so effectual a manner as to

keep them at bay. They next began to hew a pas-
sage through the door, and one of the worriors attempted to enter through the aperture; but the re-
solute mother, seizing an axe, gave him a fatal blow
upon the head, and then, with the assistance of her
daughter, drew his body in. His companions without, not apprised of his fate, but supposing him successful, followed through the same aperture, and
four of the number were thus killed before their
mistake was discovered. They now retired a few
moments, but soon returned, and renewed their exer-
tions to force the house.

"Despairing of entering by the door, they climbed
upon the roof, and made an effort to descend by the
chimney. Mr. Merrill directed his little son to
empty the contents of a large feather bed upon the
fire, which soon caused so dense a smoke, as nearly
to suffocate those who made this desperate attempt,
and two of them fell into the fireplace. The moment was critical; the mother and daughter could
not quit their stations at the door; and the husband,
although groaning with his broken leg and arm, rousing every exertion, seized a billet of wood, and with
repeated blows despatched the two half-smothered
Indians. In the mean time, the mother had repelled
a fresh assault upon the door, and severely wounded
one of the Indians, who attempted simultaneously to
enter there, while the others descended the chimney.

"Such was the character of these savages, near whom some of our people lived, and with whom our army had to contend.

"It is related of Harrison, that at the time he entered the camp he was young, slender, and apparently of a feeble constitution, and that his companions in arms, in *pity* for him, advised him to *resign his commission and go home.* But they did not know the spirit of that youthful warrior. So far from accepting their advice, he sought and soon found an opportunity to evince his energy and capacity. A train of packhorses were to be escorted to Fort Hamilton, on the Miami, a distance of twenty or thirty miles from Fort Washington. The command of this escort was given to Harrison, young as he was. The country was filled with hostile savages; and hence the undertaking was considered eminently perilous, requiring great caution and constant watchfulness. The service, however, was so successfully performed, that General St. Clair, who was still in command, expressed his especial approbation of the young ensign, and the manner in which he had discharged his commission.

"The condition of the frontier inhabitants continuing painful and alarming, General St. Clair retired from the command of the army, and was succeeded by General ANTHONY WAYNE. During the revolutionary war this officer had greatly distinguished himself. He was so impetuous as to have acquired the title of *Mad Anthony*; yet few had more discretion and sagacity. The Indians were well acquainted with his reputation, and, it is said, a knowledge of his appointment had a sensible effect on their sports. They gave him the title of *Black Snake*, from the superior cunning they ascribed to him, and even allowed him to be a match for their most distinguished warrior, Blue Jacket, or the Turtle himself.

"It was some time after his appointment before General Wayne was prepared to enter upon any decisive measures. In April, 1793, he collected his forces at Fort Washington, where Harrison, who had been raised to a *lieutenancy*, joined him. The spirit, enterprise, and energy of the latter soon attracted the notice of General Wayne, who appointed him one of the aids-de-camp, in which honorable but laborious station he continued during the remainder of the war.

"On the opening of the campaign of 1794, General Wayne prosecuted his measures with great rigor. He was determined that something decisive should be done; but before he proceeded to extremities, he resolved to try the effect of one more proposal of peace. He had in his army a man by the name of Hatch, who had long been a captive with some of the tribes, and him he selected for the hazardous enterprise.

"But Hatch did not like the scheme. He knew
the Indian temper. He was satisfied that they had
determined on war, and that even a messenger of
peace would be in danger of falling a sacrifice to
their vengeance. General Wayne, however, hoping
to bring about a peace, persuaded Hatch to go; to
which, at length, he consented, upon condition that
eight Indians, whom they had taken prisoners,
should be held as hostages, and that one Indian and
a squaw should accompany him.

"With these Hatch left the camp at four o'clock in
the afternoon, and, by travelling all night, reached
the tents of the hostile chief at daybreak the next
morning undiscovered. He immediately displayed
his flag, and proclaimed himself 'a messenger.' But
he was instantly assailed on all sides with a hideous
yell, and a call to *kill the runner! kill the spy!*

"Upon this, he accosted them in their own lan-
guage. He made known his object, at the same
time showing them General Wayne's letter, in which
he assured the chiefs that if they did not send the
bearer back to him by the sixteenth of the month,
he would at sunset of that day cause every Indian
prisoner in his possession to be put to death.

"Hatch was closely confined, and a council called
by the chiefs. On the fifteenth he was liberated,
and furnished with an answer to General Wayne,
stating, 'that if he waited where he was ten days,

and then sent Hatch for them, they would treat with him; but that if he advanced, they would give him battle.' The general's impatience had prevented his waiting the return of the messenger. On the sixteenth Hatch came up with the army on its march, and delivered the answer, to which he added, that 'from the manner in which the Indians were dressed and painted, and 'the constant arrival of parties, it was his opinion they had determined on war, and only wanted time to muster their whole force.'

"This intelligence roused the spirit of the bold and daring General Wayne, and he pressed his march down the Miami. On the 18th he reached the Rapids. On the 19th he halted within a few miles of the enemy. Early the next morning he resumed his march, and about ten o'clock his spies, who were a mile in advance, were fired upon. The army was immediately halted, and separated into two divisions. The battle soon ensued, and a hard fought battle it was. The Indians felt that upon the issue their fate depended. They knew General Wayne's spirit and impetuosity, and they fought accordingly. It was a most sanguinary conflict. The cavalry did great execution with the sabre, cutting the Indians down, until, panic-struck, they fled in confusion.

"The victory was complete for the *Long Knives*, as the Indians called the Americans, on account of their use of the broadsword. General Wayne lost in killed and wounded one hundred and thirty-three. The loss of the Indians was supposed to be much greater.

"In his official account of the engagement, General Wayne mentions with honor his *faithful and gallant aid-de-camp, Lieutenant Harrison*, as having rendered the most essential service by communicating orders in every direction, and by his conduct and bravery exciting the troops to press for victory.' This was greatly to the honor of young Harrison, and must have been highly gratifying to a youth of his spirit and ambition.

"It is related that on the evening before this battle, the Indians knowing that Wayne and his army were in the neighborhood, it was proposed in council to go forth and attack them that very night. After much deliberation, it was decided to wait till the following day. The chief called *Little Turtle* advised to make no attack at all. But *Blue Jacket* insisted that they should fight. Little Turtle had a better knowledge of Wayne than the other chiefs. He feared the man, and advised to peace. 'We have beaten the enemy,' said he at the council, 'twice, under separate commanders. We can not expect the same good fortune always to attend us. The Americans are *now* led by a chief who never *sleeps*. The night and day are alike to him; and during all the time that he has been marching upon

our villages, notwithstanding the watchfulness of our
men, we have never been able to suprise him. Think
well of it.   There is something whispers me it would
be prudent to listen to his offers of peace.'

"On this he was repproached by one of the chiefs
with cowardice, and that ended the conference.
Stung to the quick by a reproach which he was con-
scious he never merited, he would have laid the re-
viler dead at his feet; but his was not the bravery
of the assassin.   He took his post in the action, determined to do his duty; and the event proved that
he had formed no very erroneous estimate of the
character of General Wayne.

"The spirit of the Indians was broken by the
above decisive victory, and by the severe losses which
they suffered in consequence.   Not long after, they
offered to enter into negotiations for peace; and
Wayne's war, as it was called, ended on the 3d of
August, 1795, at which time a treaty was made with
them at _Greenville_, which was faithfully observed
till the battle of Tippecanoe, sixteen years after.
About this battle I shall have occasion to tell you
hereafter.

"In consequence of Harrison's services during the
campaign, and especially his gallant conduct in the
final battle, he was promoted to be a _captain_, and,
what was more honorable to him as a military man,
he was placed by General Wayne in command of

the important post, *Fort Washington.* Wayne had
here a full trial of his courage and capacity; and
though it would have been pleasant to have had him
about his person, he felt it due to Harrison, as a reward of his fidelity, and important to the interests
of the country, to give him this command. Well
did he merit the reward; and any duty which grew
out of his new station, he fulfilled with great prudence and ability.

"Being thus in a measure relieved from the perils
and uncertainties of field, or rather forest, services,
Harrison made an offer of his hand, which was accepted, to a daughter of John Cleves Symmes, the
founder of the Miami settlements, and of the city
of Ohio.

"And now," said Captain Earle, "that we have
placed our good friend in a safe and honorable station, and seen him comfortably married, we will take
leave of him for the night, hoping to renew our ac-
quaintance with him and his fortunes to-morrow
evening.

Embassy from the Indians before the Battle of Tippecanoe.

CHAPTER V.

Captain Earle tells about the Battle of Tippecanoe.

"My story, I fear, will become a tedious one before it is finished," said Captain Earle, as the family assembled the next evening. "It will be best, therefore, I think, to pass over the events of some years, and come to the battle of *Tippecanoe.* What say you, master Jose—you would like to hear about that battle?"

"Why," said Jose, "I love to hear any thing about

so brave a man as General Harrison; but I should like dearly to hear about that battle."

"I hope you won't omit any thing," said Thomas.

"I hope so, too," said William. "Have you seen any signs of weariness, father?"

"None—none," replied Captain Earle; "my audience is very attentive, and it is quite agreeable to me to prolong the story, especially as I have most of the talk to myself. But it is not necessary to be very minute on this portion of our hero's history, though he rendered very important services to the country, especially to that part called the Northwestern Territory.

"I will briefly state, then," continued Captain Earle, "that on the death of General Wayne, in 1797, Captain Harrison resigned his commission in the army, and was appointed secretary of the Northwestern Territory, in which station he acquitted himself so much to the satisfaction of the people, that as soon as they were entitled to a delegate in congress, they elected him to represent them.

"In 1800 a bill was passed in congress for dividing the Northwestern Territory. By this division, what is now the state of Ohio was made a territory by itself, and the remainder of the Northwestern Territory received the name of Indiana. At the close of the session, Harrison was appointed govenor of Indiana Territory.

"In this capacity his labors were very arduous, and very responsible. He presided over a vast territory."

"Father," interrupted Andrew, "you say this was a vast territory; did it include more than the present state of Indiana?"

"It was a much larger tract, including not only Indiana, but also what now constitutes the states of Illinois, Michigan, and the territory of Wisconsin."

Captain Earle continued. "Numerous tribes of Indians inhabited it, and it was oftentimes difficult to manage them; but Governor Harrison had had great experience. He was well acquainted with the Indian character. He had seen them, been with them, had always treated them kindly, and had gained their confidence and good-will. They loved and respected him as a father. He often entered into negotiations with them, concluded thirteen important treaties with the different tribes, and obtained for the United States not less than sixty millions of acres of their lands; fifty-one millions of which were obtained at one time. The largest tract ever ceded to our government in a single treaty.

"But I will dwell no longer on these details," said Captain Earle, "but hasten to a more important and interesting event, the *Battle of Tippecanoe*.

"This battle was fought on the 7th of November, 1811."

"Will you please first tell me, father, where Tippecanoe is situated?" asked Thomas.

"Tippecanoe is the Indian name of a river in Indiana. It is about one hundred and seventy-six miles long, and joins the river Wabash four hundred and twenty miles from its mouth."

"I thought," said Thomas, "it was the name of a town."

"Not of a town," said Captain Earle, "but of an Indian encampment, or the residence of a celebrated Indian PROPHET, who, with his equally celebrated brother TECUMSEH, was the instigator of the war. Before the details of this battle, you will like to hear something of these distinguished chiefs, and of their movements which led to it.

'TECUMSEH and ELSK-WA-TA-WA, or, as some writers spell his name, OL-LI-WA-CHI-CA, were twin brothers. It is even said that there was a trio of brothers at the same birth, and that the name of the third was KUM-SHA-KA.

"Tecumseh signifies '*The crouching Panther.*' According to Mr. Schoolcraft, *Elsk-wa-ta-wa* means '*A fire that is moved from place to place.*' But others say, it means '*The open door,*' or '*The loud voice,*' or '*Prophet.*'

, Little is known of the early years of these brothers. Their father fell in battle while they were yet mere boys. Tecumseh, it appears, gave striking evidence in his boyhood of the singular spirit which characterized him through life. He was a savage, however, of more principle than most others. He seemed to have a great regard for truth, and never indulged in the excessive use of food or liquor. He early distinguished himself as a warrior, and the love of glory was his ruling passion.

"His brother, the Prophet, was quite a different character, notorious for his cunning, and love of fraud and deception.

"About the year 1804, *Elsk-wa-ta-wa* announced himself as a prophet, and began to preach. By some it is supposed that he and Tecumseh, about this time, received the project of uniting all the western Indians against the United States, and that this plan was confirmed afterwards by the prospect of a war between this country and England.

"If such a project ever existed, the Prophet was the man to carry it forward. He had great art, and his preaching addressed itself powerfully to the Indians. He exhorted the tribes to fight no more with one another—they were brethren. He exhorted them to abandon ardent spirits, to wear skins instead of blankets, in short, to avoid imitating the whites, and to return to the more orginal manners and customs of their ancestors.

"For a time, the Prophet had little success; but, the Indians being very superstitious, and afraid of

provoking his course, they came by degrees to ac-
knowledge his pretensions.   His power became
great, and was greatly increased by his claim, that
the Great Spirit had endowed him with the ability
of seeing into the hearts of every one, and consequently he could tell who were friends, and who
were foes.   Under this pretension, several chiefs
whom he suspected were accused, and suffered death
by his order.

"I will give you an account of the death of a
celebrated Wyandot chief, known by the English
name of *Leather Lips*.   He was known to be friend-
ly to the American cause, in opposition to the English.   He was sixty-three years of age, and a most
exemplary chief.   Being suspected, the Prophet
despatched an influential chief with four other Indians to kill him.   He was found at home, and noti-
fied of the sentence which had been passed upon him.
He entreated, reasoned, and promised, but all in vain.
The messengers set about digging his grave by the
side of his wigwam.   He now dressed himself in his
finest war-clothes, and having refreshed himself with
a hasty meal, knelt down on the brink of the grave.
His executioner knelt with him, and offered up a
prayer to the Great Spirit in his behalf.   A young
Indian then approached him and struck him twice
with a tomahawk; but, finding that he still breathed,
a third blow was given, which terminated his life.

The office of burial was soon performed.

"Such was the power of this Prophet over the lives of others; and it may be added as further proof of his astonishing influence, that one of the executioners of the Wyandot chief was his *brother*.

"During the year 1807, reports came to the ears of General Harrison respecting the movements of the Indians, and especially those of the Prophet. Upon this he sent a 'Speech' to the Shawanese chiefs, couched in severe terms. Most of the chiefs being absent, the Prophet sent the following reply to Harrison :

" Father!

' I am very sorry that you listen to the advice of bad birds. You have impeached me with having corresponded with the British, and with calling and sending for the Indians from the most distant parts of the country, to listen to a fool that speaks not the words of the Great Spirit, but the words of the devil. Father! these impeachments I deny, and say they are not true. I never had a word with the British, and I never sent for any Indians. They came here themselves, to listen and hear the words of the Great Spirit.

' Father! I wish you would not listen any more to the voice of bad birds; and you may rest assured that it is the least of our idea to make disturbance, and we will rather try to stop such proceedings than encourage them.'

"This was as false as it was artful. In May or June, 1808, the Prophet took up his residence at *Tippecanoe*. Here, for two years, he continued secretly to foment jealousies and disturbances. At length, in the latter part of April, 1816, a trader, who had been for some time at the residence of the imposter, informed Governor Harrison that the Prophet had enlisted three hundred and fifty to four hundred men. About the middle of May, rumor magnified this force to six or eight hundred warriors, and the combination was said to have extended to several distant tribes.

"At length the intentions of the Prophet were fully ascertained, and the governor made prepartion to meet the rising storm.

"In the mean time, Tecumseh and the Prophet continued to urge on the Indians in their hostile feelings. They encouraged them to steal horses, plunder houses, and murder females. The whole frontier became a scene of agitation and alarm.

"Orders, at length, came from the government to Governor Harrison to move towards Tippecanoe with an armed force—but 'not to fight unless necessity required.'

"On the 28th of October the troops were put in motion from Fort Harrison, on the Wabash, about sixty miles from Vincennes, the capital of Indiana. They consisted of three hundred and fifty United States soldiers, and five hundred and fifty volunteer militia, including a squadron of dragoons, and three companies of mounted riflemen.

"On the 5th of November they encamped within nine or ten miles of the Prophet's town. On the morning following the march continued, and at the distance of three or four miles, Indians began occasionally to be seen.

"When within three miles of the town, an officer was sent forward with a flag; but, seeing a numerous party attempting to cut him off from the army, he returned. As the army approached still nearer, a counsellor of the Prophet, with two other Indians, came forth and demanded the reason of this hostile show. They stated that the Prophet wished for peace, and had sent a message to that effect by several chiefs, who had missed of meeting the governor.

"Upon this intelligence, whether true or false, the governor had no means of ascertaining, he consented to suspend hostilities, and a council was agreed upon for the following day.

"Governor Harrison, however, was on his guard. He well knew the treachery of the Indian character, and least of all had he any confidence in the Prophet. Although unwilling to believe that a night attack would be hazarded, he ordered every preparation to be made. The troops rested in their clothes, with their muskets loaded by their sides, and their bayonets fixed. The officers had their swords and sabres within reach. The governor's horse was harnessed, and ready to be mounted,

"The night passed away without disturbance. At four in the morning, the governor and his aids had risen, and were engaged in conversation before the fire. The moon was shedding a dim light through the clouds which were floating over her face. Just as the signal was about being given to the troops to rouse from their slumbers, the sound of guns was heard at a short distance, and in a moment all was motion in the camp.

"The Indians had crept close to the sentinels, with an intentions to leap upon and dispatch them. Fortunately, one of the sentinels discovered an Indian creeping through the grass, and, levelling, killed him on the spot.

"This circumstance caused the Indians to spring forward, and round the soldiers, who in a few seconds were ready for the charge. The yell was loud and terrific. The onset was desperate.

"Immediately, the night-fires of the Americans were extinguished, because they showed where the Americans were. The governor was on his horse, and passed rapidly along the line. He exorted the soldiers, and bid them fight for their wives and their children.

"The troops, animated by his presence, met the charge with corresponding valor and enthusiasm; and soon after daylight the enemy was repulsed, and such as did not fall, took hasty shelter in the recesses of a neighboring swamp.

"The American force employed amounted to about eight hundred men. Sixty-one were killed, and about double that number were wounded. The governor narrowly escaped, having the hair of his head cut by a rifle ball, which passed through the rim of his hat. The number of Indians was estimated at eight hundred or one thousand. They left thirty-eight warriors dead upon the field, besides those whom they buried in the town, who were carried thither wounded, during the battle.

"Tecumseh was absent at the time of the battle, engaged in rousing the Indians at the south. The Prophet, it is said, took no part in the engagement, but having taken a station on a neighboring eminence, employed himself in *singing a war song*.

"Thus ended the battle of Tippecanoe, in which Governor Harrison displayed the greatest energy, prudence, and sagacity. The legislature of Indiana approved his conduct in the highest terms. The assembly of Kentucky resolved, 'that for his cool, deliberate, skilful, and gallant conduct in the battle of Tippecanoe, he deserved the thanks of the nation.' President Madison, in a message to congress, said, 'Congress will see with satisfaction the dauntless spirit and fortitude victoriously displayed by every description of troops engaged, as well as the collected firmness which distinguished their commander, on an occasion requiring the utmost exertion of valor and discipline.'

"I will only add," observed Captain Earle, "that the day following was spent in taking care of the wounded, burying the dead, and fortifying the camp. The next day the dragoons were ordered to reconnoitre the town. It was found entirely deserted. Whatever was considered useful to the army was removed, after which the torch was applied to the tents, and the whole reduced to ashes.

"Thus ended the celebrated battle of Tippecanoe, from which Governor Harrison acquired the title of 'The Hero of Tippecanoe.'

"On the 7th the American troops struck their tents, and set forth on their return. The number of wounded was so great, that it was found necessary to employ every wagon to transport them. Consequently the baggage of officers and men was obliged to be destroyed. General Harrison set the example by ordering his own camp furniture to be burned. This done, the army proceeded on their march, and at length reached Vincennes, without further molestation."

Storm scene in the woods.

CHAPTER VI.

A short chapter in which Captain Earle relates some anecdotes about the "old Hero."

"I MUST pass over a good many particulars," said Captain Earle, as he resumed his narrative the next evening, "which would be interesting, had I time to relate them. But these you can read at another time, in some biography of the 'old Hero.' My object is to narrate the most important incidents in his life, and to pass rapidly on."

Here turning to William, Captain Earle inquired, "Do you recollect when the last war with England was declared?"

"I believe in 1812," replied William, "but I do not recollect the month, nor the day."

"On the 8th of June of that year," said Captain Earle. "In this war, General Harrison was destined to act a conspicuous part. No man was of more service to his country. No general had a higher reputation for bravery, skill, and perseverance. He was the idol of the northwestern army. The soldiers had the most implicit confidence in him. They knew that if they were sick, he would see them taken care of; if wounded they would not be left to suffer. If there were only a crust of bread, their general would share it with them. Where he led, they were ready to follow,—in rain, as well as in sunshine—through forests and swamps, as well as over the smooth and verdant prairie. His discipline was very strict, yet he always so contrived matters as to secure the good-will and kind feelings of his soldiers. During all his command, it is said, he never suffered a militia soldier to receive a degrading punishment. Flogging the negligent was unknown, for none were negligent; and no shooting of deserters, for none deserted.

"The happy manner in which he sometimes managed may be illustrated by an occurrence which took place at Fort Defiance, a post on the Maumee not far from Lake Erie, soon after he took command of the northwestern army.

"It was late at night when he reached the fort. Soon after he had retired to rest, he was awakened by Colonel Allen and Major Hardin, who informed him that Allen's regiment of Kentucky militia were in open mutiny, and resolved on going home. The reason assigned was, that they were exhausted by hardship, and disappointed in their expectation of an immediate engagement.

"General Harrison listened to the officers' statement, and when they had concluded, he directed them to leave the management of the case to him. That night he issued no orders, and took no further notice of the subject, except to direct an *alarm* to be beat at four o'clock in the morning.

"At four, therefore, what was the surprise of the army, as they roused from their slumbers, to hear the drums sounding an alarm. Instantly every soldier was equipped and ready for battle. The troops were ordered to form a hollow square.

"This done, General Harrison, mounted on his charger, rode up, and entered the square. The troops were surprised to see him. He had arrived in camp late the night before, and they were ignorant of the fact.

"They turned their eye upon him. Immediately

he addressed them in his usual courteous manner, rendered solemn, however, by the deep grief which the mutiny had occasioned.

"He expressed his regret that dissatisfaction and discontent had appeared, and especially among those whom he had been accustomed to regard as devoted and self-denying patriots. The war and its hardships were before them. The quiets and comforts of home were not to be found in the fields and forests, in the storms and contests, through which they must wander, and which they must experience. If, then, any were disheartened, they had liberty to retire. Turning to the regiment in which the spirit of mutiny had appeared: 'Brave Kentuckians!' said he, 'is it you who are faint-heated? You, in whose veins flows blood drawn from sires who never cowered in the field of battle? How will those sires receive you? Will you fill your wives and daughters with shame?'

"In some such terms did the gallant and warm-hearted hero address them. The appeal was irresistable. At this moment, Colonel Scott, the senior Kentucky colonel advanced and addressed his troops. 'Come,' said he, 'fellow-soldiers, give the "Hero of Tippecanoe" three cheers in token of your satisfaction, your patriotism, and determination to abide by his standard.' The voices of the soldiers in an instant broke forth into loud and long acclamations;

and from that moment no murmur was heard in the camp of Harrison, nor a wish to return home expressed.

"The hardships of the soldiers were, however, by no means imaginary. The country was new. Storms were frequent. On the cold and damp ground the soldiers were often obliged to encamp by night, with scanty provisions, and those, too, of an inferior quality.

"The expedients of General Harrison to keep up the courage and good-humor of his troops, were often most happy. One instance must suffice. Hearing that Fort Defiance was threatened with an attack from the British and Indians combined, he hastened to relieve it. On a certain night, the troops were halted at a late hour. The rain was falling in torrents. Not a tent could be pitched, the baggage not having arrived. For the same reason, no food could be procured; and only here and there a few dry sticks could be gathered with which to kindle a fire. Cold, wet, and hungry, the troops became uneasy and peevish. Harrison marked the rising storm, and, by a fortunate thought, he at once allayed it, and even diffused life and hilarity through the camp. Wrapped in his cloak, he was sitting by a dim fire, receiving the rain as it poured upon him, when suddenly turning to one of his officers. 'Come,' said he, 'give us an Irish song.'

"The officer, taking the hint, struck up :

'Now's the time for mirth and glee,
Sing, and laugh, and dance with me.'

"I do not know that the troops attempted to dance, according to this invitation," said Captain Earle, "for had they, it must have been in rain and mire ; but good-humor filled every heart, and smiles brightened up every face. In after months, when similar troubles involved the troops, and any feelings of despondency were settling upon their spirits, it was quite sufficient to dispel such clouds to sing—

'Now's the time for mirth and glee,
Sing, and laugh, and dance with me.'"

Seige of Fort Meigs.

CHAPTER VII.

Captain Earle tells about the siege of Fort Meigs, and the battle of the Thames.—Death of Tecumseh—Anecdotes.

"I HAVE this evening," said Captain Earle, "to tell you of another bold achievement of our favorite general.

"On the south side of the Maumee, a river which flows into the west end of Lake Erie, at a place called the *Rapids*, General Harrison erected a rude fort, which, in honor of Governor Meigs, of Ohio, was called *Camp Meigs, or Fort Meigs*. It was, however, strongly fortified.

"The erection of this fortification was by no means agreeable to the British, and an early plan was laid to capture and destroy it. On the 26th of April, 1813, a large party of British and Indians combined, made their appearance on the opposite side of the river. An attack now being expected, every effort was made to strengthen the place. Animated by the enthusiasm of their general, the soldiers worked with a zeal and perseverance perhaps never surpassed.

"On the evening of the 28th, the Indians were conveyed over the river in boats, and surrounded the fort in every direction.

"On the 29th, the siege began in good earnest, and all intercourse with other posts was cut off. During the preceding night the British had thrown up a mound, on which to plant their guns, and behind which they could secure themselves from the fire of the Americans.

"April 30th. Several of the Americans were this day wounded, and General Harrison himself, being continually exposed, had several narrow escapes. On the following day the enemy fired two hundred and fifty-six times from their gun batteries. The Americans fired less rapidly, but with greater effect. A bullet struck the seat on which General Harrison was sitting, and at the same time a volunteer was wounded, as he stood directly opposite to him.

"In this manner several days passed, during which both parties were engaged in firing bombs and balls, not unfrequently causing the destruction of soldiers on both sides.

"It was now doubtful what would be the issue. The pride of the British, as well as their interest, demanded the destruction of this fort. They fought, therefore, with unwonted courage and perseverance.

"In the mean while, General Harrison and his soldiers displayed the utmost coolness and determination. They were resolved to surrender only when they could fight no longer—when ammunition failed, or food and water could no longer be obtained.

"At this critical juncture intelligence was received that General Clay, with twelve hundred men, was hastening to their relief. He was already but a few miles up the river, and rapidly approaching with his troops in boats. An officer was immediately despatched, directing him to land one-half of his force on the opposite side of the river, for the purpose of forcing the enemy's batteries and spiking his cannon.

"The gallant Colonel Dudley, who was despatched for this purpose, executed the order; but, unfortunately, his troops, elated with success, pursued the retreating enemy until, suddenly, a party of Indians under command of the celebrated Tecumseh, who were in ambush, rose upon them. The slaughter was terrible.   The killed on the battle ground were horribly mutilated by the savage foe.   The brave Colonel Dudley was among the number, and more than five hundred of the detachment were taken prisoners.

"The other part of General Clay's troops were more fortunate.   They landed a short distance above the fort, and might have easily reached it ; but, lured by a party of Indians, whom they wished to destroy, they proceeded into the woods, and had not General Harrison despatched a company of cavalry to cover their retreat, they also would have been cut off.

"While these movements were in progress, several brilliant and successful charges were made from the fort.   The Americans seemed animated by the success which must crown this enterprise, if they could hold out a short time longer.

"At length the British gave up the contest.   Although they had made so great a number of prisoners, by the unfortunate management of Colonel Dudley, yet this did not aid them in relation to the fort.   Harrison would have maintained his post, had no assistance been rendered.

"The 8th of May brought an end to the toils of the Americans in the fort of Camp Meigs.   An exchange of prisoners took place, and on the morning of the 9th, the enemy commenced their retreat. Thus did Harrison sustain, in effect, a siege of twelve

days, during which the enemy had fired eighteen
hundred shells and cannon balls, besides keeping up
an almost continued discharge of small-arms The
loss of each party was about equal.

"New achievements during the war were more
remarkable than this.   The British and Indians
were more than double—yes, probably, four times
as many as were in the mud fort of Harrison.   Not
another British officer was more fierce and determined than Proctor, who commanded the siege.
And here, also, was Tecumseh, the bold and sagacious Tecumseh, and several hundred Indians,
maddened and mortified by their defeat at Tippecanoe.

"It was surprising that Harrison's courage and
that of his soldiers should have so kept up, so risen
with every succeeding day's renewed and varied
attack.

"Most wonderful," continued Captain Earle, "is
it, and most ungrateful, that there should be found
an enemy who could accuse General Harrison of
cowardice.   But such a charge has been made in
relation to his conduct at Fort Meigs.   But it has
been met as successfully as he then met the British,
and such imputations and aspersions are on the retreat as rapidly as the enemy retreated on the
morning of the 9th of May, 1813.

"I will here read you a speech of an old soldier,

Mr. Pollock, who, hearing a young man in the Ohio legislature accusing General Harrison of cowardice, rose, and shaking his hoary locks, thus rebuked the slanders of the youth:

" '*Mr. Speaker:* I have listened to the debate, thus far, with much patience. I have heard abuse heaped upon General Harrison by men who are comparatively young; and although I am unaccustomed to speech making, I hope the house will bear with me for a few moments, for I shall not trouble it long. I shall not deal in generalities; we have had too many of them already. Sir, I have heard members of this house charge General Harrison with cowardice, whom he defended and protected from the war-knife and tomahawk of the Indians, when they were sleeping in their mothers' arms.

" 'Mr. Speaker, I know something of General Harrison, and something of his history, and something of his deeds. I know individuals who were with him in the battles of the Thames, Fort Meigs, and Fort Stephenson. I know, sir, that cannon balls, chainshot, and bombshells flew thick around him in these battles. The gentleman from Clermont (Mr. Buchanan), said that General Harrison was not, during the battle of Fort Meigs, near enough to have the scales knocked off him. Well, sir, if he was not near enough to have the scales knocked off, he was near enough to have the scales

and dirt knocked on to him by cannon balls.   [Who
saw it? asked some member.]   I saw it, sir; I was
in that battle.   I saw a cannon ball strike within
two feet of General Harrison during that fight.   I
was there.   I saw bombshells and chainshot flying
all around him.   Horses were shot down under him.
I was also at the battle of Fort Stephenson.   I saw
General Harrison there, and he was in the hottest
and hardest of the fight ; and where balls flew thickest, and where steel blushed the fiercest, there would
you find General Harrison.   I speak what I know,
and what my eyes have seen.   General Harrion is
not a coward ; and those who call him a coward
know nothing of him.   He was a brave, prudent,
and fearless general.   He took the right course
during the last war; he acted a noble part, and his
country has honored him for it.   Ask the soldiers
who fought by his side ; whose arms were nerved
by his presence ; whose hearts were cheered by his
valor; and who were led to triumph and to victory
by his courage, and bravery, and skill, if General
Harrison was a coward ; and they, sir, will tell you
No !

   " 'Sir, I have done.   I only wished to give my
testimony in favor of General Harrison, and to
state what I have seen, in opposition to those who
are ignorant of his character, and who   now nothing of his bravery and skill.'

"The decisive victory thus obtained at Fort Meigs," continued Captain Earle "sent a thrill of joy through the land, almost equal to that which in the revolution was awakened by the triumph of Saratoga. It dispelled the gloom which prevaded the nation. It turned the tide of war, and led directly to other splendid achievements, which not long after, decided the contest on the northeastern frontier.

"Of these other achievements, I have time to notice but one, and that briefly, the 'BATTLE OF THE THAMES.'

"The Thames is a river in Upper Canada, flowing into Lake St. Clair. On the 5th of October, a severe battle was fought near this river between the Americans under General Harrison, and the British and Indians, the former led by General Proctor, and the latter by Tecumseh. The Americans were speedly and decisively victorious, making six hundred prisoners and putting the rest of the enemy to flight. Here was the last struggle of the renowned Tecumseh. Disdaining to fly, while all were flying around him but his own nearest followers, he pressed eagerly into the heat of the contest, encouraging the savages by his voice, and plying the tomahawk with tremendous energy.

"But he fell—by whose hand it is not certainly known. The honor, if it may be called an honor,

was claimed by *Colonel Johnson*. But it was no
ordinary man that there fell—savage that he was.
Like Philip, of Mount Hope, at an earlier date, he
was terrible in battle. His ruling maxim in war was
to take no prisoners. He neither gave any quarters,
nor accepted any. A writer remarks of him, 'that
his carriage was erect and lofty. His eloquence was
nervous and concise. Habitually taciturn, his words
were few, but always to the purpose.'

" It is an interesting fact that 'the grave in which
Tecumseh's remains were deposited by the Indians
after the return of the American army, is still visible
near the borders of a willow marsh, on the north
line of the battle ground, with a large fallen oak
tree lying beside. The willow and wild rose are
thick around it, but the mound itself is cleared of
shrubbery, and is said to owe its good condition to
the occasional visits of his countrymen. Thus re-
pose, in solitude and silence, the ashes of the INDIAN
BONAPARTE.' In truth have they

      ·Left him alone in his glory.' "

"Father," inquired Andrew, "what became of the
Prophet?"

"I know not his particular history after the battle
of Tippecanoe. Some author, I think, relates that he
died only a few years since. After the above battle, he had very little influence, and I believe very

little agency in the war. Both Tecumseh and the Prophet received an annual pension from the British government.

"Let us return a few moments to General Harrison.

"It was his practice—quite different from that of some commanders—to favor himself in nothing, but to share with his common soldiers their toils and deprivations. This greatly endeared him to them, and to this day, wherever a soldier is found, however humble, who, followed the fortunes of General Harrison, he will be hard to extol him.

"A pleasant anecdote is related of him while in pursuit of General Proctor up the Thames. A single valise contained the whole of his baggage, while a blanket thrown over his saddle served him for a bed; or rather the ground was his bed, and the blanket his only covering. Yet even this blanket he gave away to Colonel Evans, a British officer, who was wounded and a prisoner, because he needed it more than himself! Such humanity—such self-denial, is rare.

"The night following the battle of the Thames, thirty-four British officers, prisoners of war, supped with him. But the camp, especially after a battle, afforded little variety. Indeed, it is said that the general was able to give them only some fresh roasted beef, without bread, and without salt. The sol-

diers had the same, their fare was always like that
of their general. Whatever luxuries he had, they
had; and whatever hardships, difficulties, and dan-
gers they encountered, he shared them with his
troops. When the morning arrived, and their
slumbers were broken up by the rattling drum, he
was out and mounted on his horse. When the
storm beat upon them, he breasted it himself. When
they were dispirited, his cheerfulness wore away
the gloom. When they were sick, or were wounded
in the service of their country, he saw that their
wants were supplied.

"Few commanders were ever more beloved, or
more readily obeyed than General Harrison; and
the secret of this affection and control lay in his
uniform kindness. One instance of kindness must
serve as a specimen of hundreds of others which
might be related. A regiment was on the point of
leaving Vincennes for the northwestern frontier.
At the moment of their departure, advancing towards
them, he said: 'If you ever come to Vincennes, you
will always find a plate and knife and fork at my
table; and I can assure you that you will never find
the string to the latch of my door pulled in.'"

"Father," inquired Jose, "what is meant by a
string to a latch? I never saw a latch with a string to
it."

"Formerly," replied Captain Earle, "the people

had wooden latches, because such latches as we have were quiet rare, or they were unable to purchase them. A string tied to a wooden latch was passed through a hole in the door. This string being pulled, raised the latch; when drawn in, no one on the outside could open the door. In the western country, such latches are probably common in the 'log cabins,' and perhaps at that time such a latch was on the door of the log cabin in which General Harrison lived.

De Wood Leg Soldiare, etc.

CHAPTER VIII.

Captain Earle spends an evening in telling anecdotes about General Harrison.

"I HAD no intention, my children," Captain Earle remarked the succeeding evening, as he was taking his seat, "I had no intention when I began these notices of the 'Hero of Tippecanoe,' of extending them to so great a length. But the subject is fruitful, and the half has not yet been told.

"But I must not be tedious, and will therefore give the remaining history of the general in few words.

76

"In 1814, he resigned his commission in the army. This resignation was in consequence of arrangements made by the secretary of war, by which General Harrison was still to retain his commission, but not be employed in active service. To this he could not consent. He loved the excitement of the field. His patriotic spirit could then find grateful exercise only in conducting the soldiers whom he had trained into the field of action. As another, through the prejudice of the secretary, was appointed to do this, General Harrison retired from the army.

"Two years after, he was elected a member of congress, subsequently a member of the state senate of Ohio, and, in 1824, a senator of the United States. In 1828, President Adams appointed him minister to the republic of Colombia, in South America. In these various situations he proved himself most useful to his country, adding to his reputation as a statesman honors beyond those which he had acquired as a soldier.

"Returning at length to his country, he retired to a farm at *North Bend*, on the banks of the Ohio, fifteen or twenty miles below Cincinnati. Here, contented with the honors acquired by years of patriotic devotion to his country, he has lived, employing himself in rural occupations, and at the same time gathering from the soil his support, which others, if not more selfish, yet more careful of their own interests, have secured from the emoluments of office."

"Do you mean, father," inquired William, "to say that General Harrison is poor?"

"I believe," replied Captain Earle, "that he is by no means rich. It has been stated, that for his services as commander of the expedition to Tippecanoe, he never asked and never received any compensation. As commander of the northwestern army, his expenses so far exceeded his pay, that subsequently he was obliged to sell a fine tract of land to meet them."

"Does General Harrison live in a log cabin?" asked Thomas.

"So it is reported—a log cabin, which, within a few years, has been covered and painted white. The house is large, with a noble lawn, large trees, and a fine view of the river. It is said to be plain, but extremely neat."

"You have not told us how General Harrison looks," observed Thomas.

"In person he is tall and slender. His eye is dark, and remarkable for its expression. No one could see him and not be convinced of his intelligence; no one can read the history of his life, and not be satisfied of the benevolence of his heart. In his manners he is plain, easy, and unostentatious. In disposition he is generous, in temper, mild and forbearing, strong in his attachments, forgiving towards his enemies.

Here, pausing and taking some papers from the table, Captain Earle observed, that he had marked several interesting anecdotes concerning the general, a few of which it will give you pleasure, I presume, to hear. Here is one entitled

"BOYS, DO YOU HEAR THAT?"

"Twenty-six years ago last autumn," said the gentleman who related the anecdote, "I was a boy attending school in a log cabin, with no other windows than the light afforded through the space of two logs, by the removal of a piece of the third, with greasy bits of paper pasted on as substitutes for glass. The cabin, dedicated to learning, was situated in the outskirts of a now populous town in Pennsylvania. No state in the Union furnished more or better soldiers for the defence and protection of the northern frontier of Ohio, during the late war, than did Pennsylvania. Not a few of her sons were in the army surrendered by Hull; besides, numbers of her brave fellows were massacred and scalped at Winchester and Dudley's defeat. Still, the after-call of General Harrison for more soldiers was answered by large numbers of Pennsylvanians, including several from our village. The departure of these brave fellows from their families and friends, was *then* viewed as voluntary sacrifice of life for the defence of their country; and the 'farewell, God bless ye!' was uttered in a tone and feeling that

sunk deep in the hearts of the bystanders, and which
will never be effaced from my memory.

"In these days, our mails were few and uncer-
tain; and it was only by the occasional passing of
a sick or disabled soldier returning home, that we
heard from our army. Time hung heavy, and deep
gloom overspread our country. The last news was,
'A battle is soon expected between the American
army under General Harrison, and the British and
Indians under the bloodthirsty *Proctor* and *Tecumseh!*"

"Days and weeks passed by, and yet nothing was
heard from our army. The citizens eagerly hailed
all strangers from the West, with the anxious inquiry of, 'Any news from General Harrison?' Such
was the delay, doubt, and uncertainty, that it was
generally feared, and by many believed, that Harrison and his army had, like those before him, been
defeated and massacred.

"While I was sitting, said the Gentleman, "at the
long low window of our schoolhouse, and our Irish
schoolmaster was busy in repeating our A B C to
the smaller urchins, I suddenly heard the sound of a
horn. I looked forth, and saw descending the hill,
half a mile distant, the mail boy on a horse at full
speed. At the foot of the hill, he crossed the bridge,
and the rapid clatter of the iron hoof resounded
throughout our cabin. Rising the hill near us, his

horse at full speed, and reeking with sweat, he again
sounded his shrill horn, and, when opposite our log
cabin, he called out:

"'HARRISON HAS WHIPPED THE BRITISH AND
INDIANS!'

"Our Irish tutor, with as true an *American* heart
as ever beat in a son of Erin, sprang from his seat
as though he had been shot, his eyes flashing with
fire, he screamed out:

'BOYS, DO YOU HEAR THAT ?'

"He caught his hat, darted out at the door, and
followed the mail-boy at the top of his speed. The
scholars were not a second behind him—the larger
ones taking the lead, and shouting '*Huzza for Harrison!*' and the smaller ones running after, halloing
and screaming with fright!

"The people of our village hearing the confusion,
and seeing the mail-boy and horse at full run, followed by the schoolmaster at the top of his speed, and
his whole school screaming—shouting and screaming—knew not what to make of it. The mechan-
ic left his shop—the merchant his store—and the
women stretched their necks out of the windows,
while consternation and dismay were depicted on
every countenance. The mail arriving at the office,
the carrier rose in his stirrups, and exclaimed, at the
same time whirling his hat in the air:

"'HUZZA FOR HARRISON! HE HAS WHIPPED THE BRITISH AND INDIANS!'

'BOYS, DO YOU HEAR THAT?'

"A universal shout of joy involuntarily burst forth, bonfires were kindled in the streets, and our village was illuminated at night."

HARRISON AND THE ASSASSIN.

"I have related the particulars of the battle of Tippecanoe. One incident I have reserved for the present time. The evening before the battle, a negro was seen to enter the American camp, and cautiously steal towards the general's marque. His conduct was so suspicious that he was arrested, and at the time of the action was a prisoner in the camp. After the battle a court-martial was ordered, of which Colonel Boyd was appointed president.

"On the trial, it was proved that he had deserted from the American camp, and that, instigated by the Indians, he had returned with the intention of murdering the governor while asleep. With this guilt upon him, he was sentenced to suffer death within an hour. But General Harrison, after he had approved the sentence, was reluctant to give the fatal order.

" 'If he had been out of my sight,' said General Harrison, when afterwards relating the circumstance,

'he would have been executed; but when he was
first taken, General WELLS and Colonel OWEN, who
were old Indian fighters, as we had no irons to put
on him, had secured him after the Indian fashion.
This is done by throwing a person on his back, split-
ting a log and cutting notches in it to receive the
ankles; then replacing the several parts, and com-
pressing them together with forks driven over the
log into the ground. The arms are extended and
tied to stakes secured in the same manner. The
situation of a person thus placed, is as uneasy as can
possibly be conceived. The poor wretch thus confined, lay before my fire, his face receiving the rain
that occasionally fell, and his eyes constantly turned
upon me, as if imploring mercy. I could not with-
stand the appeal, and I determined to give him
another chance for his life. I had all the commis-
sioned officers assembled, and told them that his fate
depended on them. Some were for executing him,
and I believe a majority would have been against
him, but for the interference of the gallant SNELLING.
'Brave comrades? said he, 'let us save him. The
wretch deserves to die, but as our commander, whose
life was more particularly his object, is willing to
spare him, let us also forgive him. I hope, at least,
that every officer of the fourth regiment will be on
the side of mercy.' SNELLING prevailed, and BEN
was discharged."

THE OLD SOLDIER.

"I was dining with General Harrison in the spring of 1839," said a gentleman, "and while in the midst of our repast, a loud knock was heard at the door. My host rose from the table, excused himself, and went to the door to see who it was that was so desirous of admittance. After a parley of some moments with a person who spoke in a rough tone of voice, the general ushered into the room a very old man, whose worn-out and tattered garments bespoke great distress and poverty.

" 'Mr. ——,' said Gen. Harrison, ' this is one of my old soldiers, and I have invited him in to dine with us. He was with me in the sortie of Fort Meigs and at the Thames. I remember his bravery well. There are the men whom we must honor. Take that seat, George.'

"George, for that was the old soldier's name," continued our friend, "sat down and soon gave us cause to know that a good dinner and he had been strangers for many a long day. The old fellow's feelings became enlivened by the good things he had partaken of, and a glass or two of whisky and water, and for nearly two hours, did the general and he fight their battles over again. Towards evening, the general took me aside and asked me to join with him in the charity he was about to bestow. I cheerfully consented. The general went to his bedroom, and in a few moments returned with a new black coat.

"'George,' said the hero, 'this is the only coat I have except the threadbare one on my back. Take it, and while it protects you from the inclement winds of our cold spring, remember, that had your old general his way, every old soldier in the country should not know what want was the rest of his days.'

"I added my mite to George's empty purse, and gave him 'silver' enough to carry him home into the interior of Ohio—for he had been to New Orleans on a flat-boat and was now on his return."

"'You will take this note,' said the General, 'and when you go to Cincinnati, call on Mr. M——; give him this, and he will further aid you. I am like yourself, George, poor, and have to labor for my living, after long toil and hard work in the service of my country, but we poor soldiers enjoy at least the proud consciousness of having done our duty.'

"After some further conversation, George departed, thanking his old general from his heart. This little circumstance turned the conversation between the general and myself upon the hardships of the last war, the faithfulness of his troops, and the true policy that the government ought to pursue to its surviving defenders. This anecdote, however, will serve to show you the kind-hearted goodness of the old general, and it proves that if he is elected president, he will be the president of the people—accessible to all."

An Irishman by the name of John Hanley emigrated a few years since to Cincinnati, Ohio, with his young wife. He had married her contrary to the wishes of her father, which was the cause of his leaving his country.

On his arrival in Cincinnati, he opened a small store, by means of which he was able to support himself and wife. At length intelligence reached him that his father in Ireland was dead, and had left him a handsome share of his property. Upon this, he immediately sold his effects, and with his wife embarked for his native country. But on reaching the place of his birth, what was his disappointment to find that the whole sum left him was only five pounds!

No sooner had he learned what unkindness had been practiced by his father, than, raising a small sum, he again returned to Cincinnati. His wife being an accomplished woman, endeavored to aid her husband by giving lessons in music.

The story of their disappointment reached the ears of General Harrison. He felt interested in them, as he has ever been interested in the sorrows and trials of the unfortunate. Just at that time, there was a clerkship in his office vacant. It was worth five hundred dollars a year. Many personal friends of General Harrison solicited it of him in behalf of their sons. But he refused them all, and gave the place to Hanley, the poor young Irishman.

Hanley's gratitude can not well be imagined. He entered upon his duties, and while health lasted, he was contented and happy. But he fell sick, and for the last six months of his life he was unable to perform the duties of his station. But mark the kindness of Harrison. He contrived to have the duties performed. and Hanley or his wife was paid to the day of his death.

Such kindness is as beautiful as it is rare. A heart in which such sympathy dwells, is not likely to lose its generous tendencies, whatever honors or offices are bestowed upon its possessor. How desirable to have such a man at the head of the nation, rather than one who has little more sensibility to the woes of others than marble, and can no more sympathize with the sons and daughters of misfortune than an iceberg !

"DE WOOD LEG SOLDIARE."

"Are you personally acquainted with General Harrison ?" asked an American of a French traveller.

"Begare, sare." replied the Frenchman, "I have

de grand satisfactiong to have the plaisare, sare, to have de grand introductiong, sare, to the brave hero and citizen. I make you introductiong, sare, to this gentilhomme, who will tell de grand story of de old shenerall, and de wood leg soldiare. It is ver good."

This appeal was made to a respectable-looking. gentleman—a clergyman—who remarked that it would give him pleasure to tell the story.

He related as follows:

It was in the year 1820, if my memory is correct, that I was traveling in Ohio with a view of purchasing a tract of land for my son, when I fell in with a gentleman who was a stranger, and whom I found a very intelligent and agreeable companion. A thunder storm drove us into a neat log cabin, a litttle distance from the road-side, for shelter, where we found a house full of children. a sick and very interesting-looking woman lying on an humble but clean-looking bed, and a young, pretty maiden sitting near. The husband and father, with a wooden leg, and a deep scar across his brow, was bending over the bed and pressing the hand of the sick woman between both of his. His eyes were intently fixed on a young infant, apparently a few months old. The whole group had been indulging in tears, and I saw one stealing from the dazzling eyes of the young damsel as she sat listening apparently to some tale of woe which her father told. The tears were suddenly wiped away as we approached, and were given a cordial welcome.

"You seem to be in distress," said the stranger, my companion.

"I have faced the enemies of my country," said the host, as he swung his wooden leg round to close the door, "and I have felt all the pangs and privations of a military life, but all this was nothing compared with what I have suffered to-day."

Stranger. Pardon me if I ask the cause; for I will relieve you if it lies in my power.

Host. My wife is afflicted with an internal disease, which renders it dangerous to move her; yet, for a debt which I cannot immediately raise, the man who is agent for another, declares that if I do not pay it before to-morrow at twelve o'clock, he will seize what little I possess, and turn us all out to the mercy of the elements. I can neither raise the sum by that time, nor obtain a shelter for my poor wife and children, who must perish to gratify the malice of a man whose heart is a stranger to mercy.

The whole family melted into tears as he concluded, and even the soldier himself, who had faced the cannon's mouth, could not refrain from weeping.

Stranger. You have fought the battles of the country? May I be inquisitive in asking—

Host. Oh! yes, I fought under the brave Harrison at the Thames and in other battles. I speak of him with pride, for I have seen his sword glittering in the thickest of the fight.

Stranger. Would you know him were you to see him ?

Host (gazing in his face). You resemble him very much. Were he to know my sufferings, he would instantly assist me. I have seen him do several generous deeds.

Stranger. Where did you lose your leg ?

Host. It was shattered by a ball at the glorious battle of Tippecanoe.

Stranger. Well, my brave fellow, make your mind easy; a hair of your head shall not be injured. You now see your general before you, and as you have fought for me and your country, I will now protect you and your family at the risk of my life.

A sudden blaze of joy seemed to run from heart to heart; the soldier clasped General Harrison in his arms, while the children pressed his hand with affection.

"We shall be saved from ruin," cried the pale wife.

The general found the owner of the piece of land on which the soldier lived, and never rested until he made the poor fellow a right to it. He also discharged the debt, and a happier family I never beheld.

HARRISON AND THE METHODIST MINISTER.

General Harrison was sitting one summer evening
at the door of his "log cabin." It had been an in-
tensely warm day, and here he was sitting with the
hope of getting cool after the labors of the day, when
a man approached and solicited a shelter for the
night.

The jaded appearance of the steed, and the soiled
garments of the rider, proclaimed the fatigue of the
day, and with his usual courtesy, the old general
welcomed the stranger. After a plain and substantial
supper, the guest joined with his host in social conversation; and the latter, laying aside the character
of the soldier and statesman, willingly listened to the
pious instructions of the traveler, whom he discovered
to be a minister of the gospel.

They retired to rest, the good old soldier thankful
to a munificent Providence that he was enabled to
administer to the wants of a fellow creature, and the
worthy minister of Christ, invoking the blessing of
heaven upon the head of his kind benefactor.

Morning came, and the minister prepared to depart. He was in the act of taking leave, when he
was informed that his horse had died during the
night. The loss, however severe, considering that
he had yet two hundred miles to travel, did not dis-
courage him in the exercise of his duty; but taking
his saddle-bags on his arm, he rose to depart, with

thanks for the kindness of his entertainer. The old
general did not attempt to detain him, though he offered his condolence upon the loss; but an observ-
ing eye could have detected a smile of inward satisfaction, which the consciousness of doing good alone
produces. The guest reached the door, and to his
astonishment, found one of the general's horses, ac-
coutred with his own saddle and bridle, in waiting
for him. He returned and remonstrated, stating
his inability to pay for it, and that in all probability
he should never again visit that section of the country. But the general was inexorable, and reminded
the astonished divine that "he who giveth to the
poor lendeth to the Lord"—sent him on his way,
his heart overflowing with gratitude, and his prayers
directed to heaven for the blessings of the venerable
hero.

Harrison elected by Captain Earle's family.

CHAPTER IX.

The "Hero of Tippecanoe" elected president by Captain Earle and his family.

At the conclusion of the anecdotes the evening before, as it was late, the children retired without learning whether their father intended to gratify them with any further account of the "old hero."

At breakfast, therefore, the inquiry was made with some solicitude.

"You have been pleased, then, my children, with

the manner in which we have spent some evenings
past ?"

"Very greatfully," said one.   "Highly," said another.   "I hope you have not finished," said Thomas.

"Let us hear what Jose wishes," said Captain
Earle.

"I'm sure I love to hear stories," said Jose ; "but
you haven't told us certainly whether General Harrison is to be the next president."

"That is more than I know," said Captain Earle,
"but I think he will, and every day confirms me in
the opinion.   But I design to spend one evening
more in talking on this subject, and then we will wait
patiently till the question is settled."

The family here separated for the day.   The sons
were soon at school, Mrs. Earle engaged in her
usual domestic avocations, and the captain abroad
on business in a neighboring town.

I will not say that the day was a long one to the
children, but they appeared quite pleased, when, tea
being finished, and the table occupying its usual place,
they gathered once more to listen to their father.

"The remarks which I am about to make to you
this evening, my children," Captain Earle began,
"are rather of a grave character ; but as they are
connected with the 'old hero,' and the welfare of
the country, you will find them, I hope, interesting.

"We are now on the eve of a new presidential election. In a few months the states will vote for electors of president and vice-president. Each state chooses as many electors as it sends representatives to congress. The electors meet in the several states, and give their votes. These votes are sealed up, and sent to Washington, where, in the month of February, they are opened in the presence of congress, and the candidate who has the majority of all the votes is declared to be president of the United States for four years.

"The candidate who shall be elected next autumn, will take his oath of office on the 4th day of March, 1841.

"The office of president of the United States is a high and honorable office. The salary attached to it is greater than that of any other office in the government; and the influence of the president is greater, perhaps, than that of ony other man. The nation provides a large and splendid house for him, and furnishes it with elegant and costly furniture.

"The people take a deep interest in the question, 'Who will be president?' Such an interest they ought to feel. The Bible says, 'When the righteous are in authority, the people rejoice; but when the wicked beareth rule, the people mourn.'

"Rulers have great influence. The president of the United States, from his station and power, can accomplish good or evil for the nation. If he be a wise, a prudent, and a good man—one who loves the happiness and welfare of the people more than his private interest—the nation will be happy and prosperous. Business will thrive. Industry will be encouraged. Men will find employment; they will be able to support their families. Children will have good clothes and good food. There will be schools, and the means of paying teachers.

"On the other hand, if a selfish and ambitious man is made president, he will regard his own interests more than those of the people. His ends must be served. His ambitious views must be carried out. No matter whether the country is prosperous, no matter whether business thrives—whether the laborer gets good wages, or children are well fed or well educated. These are considerations of small moment with a selfish and wicked president. His object is attained, if he can retain his office— get his $25,000 a year—be praised and flattered —ride in his splendid coach with fine horses, and eat his good dinners on gold or silver plate. When such a man rules, the people *do mourn*.

"No wonder, then, that the people of the United States feel a deep interest in the question, 'Who is to be president?' Every man, woman, and child has such an interest, as the manner in which he administers the government may affect generations unborn.

While, then, no one should use unlawful means to prevent the election of any candidate, every one is justified, and even bound by duty, to exert his influence in all lawful and honorable ways to secure the election of the man who will look well to the good of the country, and who will take care of the *poor* as well as the *rich*, and of children as well as of persons who have attained to manhood. This is my creed, and the true creed, I believe, of the real patriot.

"Since the year 1789 we have had eight different presidents—George Washington, John Adams, Thomas Jefferson, James Madison, James Monroe, John Quincy Adams, Andrew Jackson, and Martin Van Buren, who is president at this time. Until within a few years, we have been a prosperous and happy people—no nation more so; but in 1829, or soon after, a great change came over the country. In that year, Andrew Jackson entered upon the presidency. He promised to administer the government so that the prosperity of the people should continue; but whether he was unable, or self-willed, or from some other cause, the prosperity of the country began to decline. He entered upon *new experiments*, which failed, and left the money matters of the country in great derangement and confusion.

"Mr. Van Buren has managed as badly, and even worse than President Jackson. He said that he would follow his measures, and he has done so. General Jackson turned the ship of state out of her course, and Mr. Van Buren has kept on. He has been admonished of danger—been told by several good old pilots that he would run the ship aground or drive her on breakers, where she would be ship-wrecked. But he has seemed to fear no evil and to listen to no counsel.

"Thus the country suffers. Business is nearly sus-pended—confidence is destroyed. Thousands, who were rich, have become poor, and the poor are beg-ging. If affairs long continue as they are now, I hope, my children, that I shall be able to procure you *bread*, but the *comforts* which you have enjoyed must be dimimished. I cannot pay for books—I cannot educate you.

"It is so now, or will soon be so, with thousands in all the land.

"What shall be done? One expedient remains: we must alter the course of the ship. If Mr. Van Buren is re-elected, he tells us he will not alter it, but will still follow in the *'steps of his illustrious predecessor.'*

"If we would change, then, our course, we must change our captain, our commander. General Har-rison, the 'Hero of Tippecanoe,' the plain, honest. but intelligent, straight-forward, good old-fashioned farmer of Ohio, is recommended as *the man*. He *is*

a man—an *honest* man, 'the noblest work of God'—
and he is *the* man who comes recommended from all
quarters of the land.　The spirit of reform is abroad
in the nation.　'The *people* are coming.'　If I live,"
said Captain Earle, "till the time of voting, *I* will
vote for *General William Henry Harrison.*"

"I wish I could vote, father," said William.

"I wish so too," said Captain Earle.　"Were it
right, I would wish to see all my boys at the ballot-
box."

"Some doubt, I suppose," said William, "how
Andrew would vote."

"I would vote with a good conscience," said Andrew, "or not vote at all."

"It has just occurred to me," said Captain Earle,
"that there can be no harm in taking the question
here to-night, 'Who shall be president?'"

"Will our vote decide who will be president?" asked Jose.

"It will decide whom *we wish should be.*"

"I like the plan well," said William.　"As William Henry Harrison is a prominent candidate, and
that is my name, who can tell but that I may be run
in president this very evening."

"Well," said Captain Earle, "you may prepare
your votes."

"I don't know how," said Jose; "I can not
write."

"Well, Jose," said Captain Earle, "there are thousands who vote for president, who can neither *read*, *write*, nor *spell*, nor *scarcely think*. You must get some one to write for you."

"Well, I'll get *mother* to write me a vote. Mother, will you?"

"It is not often," said Mrs. Earle, "that *ladies* write votes; but I will oblige you. Come and whisper the name you wish me to write."

Jose whispered, and Mrs. Earle laughed outright.

"Why, ladies don't *vote*, my son," said his mother.

"What is that?" inquired Captain Earle. "Surely, we must all be pleased to know what pleases mother so much."

"Why, Jose wishes me," said Mrs. Earle, "to write the same name for him that I do for myself."

"Good, my son," said Captain Earle; "that is a capital thought. We must have your mother's vote also."

"Well," said Andrew, "I am agreed. I presume mother will vote for *Mr. Van Buren*, as he is quite a *lady's man*."

"Andrew," said Mrs. Earle, "your mother would wish that a president of the United States should be a *gentleman;* but something more is requisite to govern a people well, than to know how to *bow* and *simper* in a *drawing-room*."

"Ah!" said Andrew, "I see how all the world are going. If the *ladies* are opposed to Mr. Van Buren, there is little chance for the re-election of my successor."

"Come, prepare your votes," said Captain Earle, "I am quite impatient to have the question settled."

"Mother," said Jose, "won't you vote?"

"I have prepared two votes," said Mrs. Earle. "Perhaps, however, you would prefer that your father should write one for you."

"I guess father and mother will vote for the same candidate," said Jose; "for I have heard you say, that husband and wife must pull at the same end of the rope."

"Quite smart, Jose, and quite true," said Captain Earle. "Are you all ready? Come, Jose, you hand round the *ballot-box*."

"We haven't any ballot-box," said Jose.

"Well, take that little basket. Don't put in *two* votes—*one* vote *each*."

"Here, Jose, hand it to your mother first," said Captain Earle.

"To your father next," said Mrs. Earle.

"Now bring the basket to me. Have all voted?"

"No," said, Jose, "I haven't put my vote in."

"Well, hand in your vote, as they say at the electors' meeting. All in? all voted? the box—I mean the *basket*—is ready to be closed. One minute more—only one. *The box is closed.*"

"Now let us count. The first vote is for William Henry Harrison; the second, William Henry Harrison the third, same; the fourth, same; the fifth, same; the sixth—"

Captain Earle paused. "The sixth—"

"Ah!" said William, "that's *Andrew's* vote—for whom is it?"

"You are not certain that it is Andrew's—it may be your mother's."

"Well, for whom is it, father? Pray, let us know."

"The sixth is for—for—for— *William Henry Harrison!*"

"Good! good!" exclaimed Thomas.

"Yes, good it is, good enough," said Captain Earle. "I hope the autumnal election will tell as well as ours has to-night!"

"I wish the ladies might *all* vote," said Jose, "mother has voted so well."

"I suspect, my son," said Mrs. Earle, "if the *ladies* had a voice in the matter they would vote for some one who would so manage that their husbands and children should have *food and clothing.*"

"Good times after this," said William. "Under *my administration* I hope you will have food and clothes, and in abundance. Andrew, I thank you for your vote."

"Why," said Andrew, "you know I could not

well vote for myself, Billy ; and as to *my successor*
in office, he didn't manage as well as I expected,
and I myself believe he may with advantage to the
country return to *Kinderhook.*"

"I hope he may," said Captain Earle, "most sin-
cerely I do, and that *his* successor may be

> 'The iron-hearted soldier, the true-hearted soldier,
> The gallant old soldier of Tippecanoe!' "

We who know the result of the election of 1841, can thus
endorse the old saying that 'many a true word is spoken in
jest.'

Review of the Life of Gen. Benjamin Harrison

CHAPTER X.

"Some men are born great—some achive greatness—some have greatness thrust upon them."—Twelfth Night.

One of the greatest perogatives of this glorious republic, is the fact, that no matter how lowly a citizen of it may be born, he has the chance of ultimately holding the proudest position that the world can offer, viz, the Presidency of the United States; and if we trace back through the history of this country, we shall find the record of many presidents, who began life at the bottom rung of the ladder.

In giving a review of the life of our President, we find such a one, who commenced life as a poor man, and who, by dint of energy and pluck, has raised himself to that piniele of fame, which makes him the envy and admiration of his fellow men.

Born in his grandfather's house at North Bend, Ohio, on the 20th of August, 1833, his boyhood was spent in this out of the way spot, until he went to Farmer's College, where he stayed two years; and when transferred from there to Miami University, he was so well endowed in his studies and general information, as to at once enter as Junior, in the latter institution. So much has been said about the "Log Cabin" that we cannot refrain from describing the birth place of General Harrison. There is a tongue of land nearly five miles long, extending southward from the old Harrison home-stead, at North Bend, its lower part touching the boundary line of Indiana, the north side, is swept by the Miami River, whilst the Ohio rolls placidly by on the southern side. On the peninsula, as some might call it, is what was the farm of John Scott Harrison; father of "Our President," who was reckoned a good farmer; for whatever else he might have been, he could certainly lay claim to understanding how to farm his land. Had it not been for his generosity, and a judgment too easily cheated, by people who wormed their way into his confidence, he might have left his family provided for at his death; but as it was, through his good nature, he left no estate. For prior to his death, the heirs of Judge Short took posession of his farm, and it was through their kindness and out of the great respect they bore him, that he was allowed to continue in its occupancy. His house fronted the Ohio River; the dining room which was the common sitting room, was large and commodious, with the usual wide open fire-place; in this room it was the custom of the family to assemble, particularly in the winter evening, around a central table; light was obtained from the old fashioned tallow dips, aided by the flame from the fire place; in front of which the mother would sit knitting socks for the boys and listening to the conversation, or reading, of the younger folks. Be-

tween the river and the house was a small old fashioned
log school house; this cabin was, as is usual with such build-
ings of the very plainest, the floor being formed of punch-
con, and having windows small and few; the great fire place
was at one end, and being filled with logs in the morning
would thus last all day; for seats, there were benches,
without backs, formed of slabs, with supports of sticks fitted
in through auger-holes. It was in this lowly cabin, that
young Harrison commenced his education; his time being
taken up in seasons when the crops were being planted, or
harvested, with such employment as was suitable to him, as
a farmer's boy of his age. For amusement there was fishing
and hunting, the rivers close by being well stocked with
fish, while squirrels were plentiful in the woods, and in
their season ducks were very abundant; Benjamin was an
expert shot, particularly with the rifle.

A custom handed down from the first General Harrison
when at home, was to invite the congregation of the Church
to the old homestead, where often plates for fifty or more
were laid. and on such occasions the board was profusely
covered with the good things of this life; every thing being
the product of the farm. When at the Miami University,
young Harrison met the daughter of president Scott, a
young lady, described as being girlish, intelligent, witty
and attractive, and too whom he became engaged, she being
all that went to make up his ideal of a perfect women, and
to whom, on the 20th of October, 1853, he was married.
He then went to live with his wife, at his father's place
where he continued to study We next find him, looking
out for a place, where he could begin life, as a bread-win-
ner, and after serious consideration, he at last decided, that
Indianapolis was the spot, where he went for that purpose
in March, 1854, and in which place, he has resided ever
since.

He was barely twenty-one, when he settled there with his wife; with little of this world's goods to call his own, but he had a good education, and determined to make the law his profession, his fortune consisted of the sum of $800; money advanced on a piece of property he had inherited from an Aunt who married James Finley, a soldier of the war of 1812, and who left her a widow; this sum was not large enough to purchase a house, or rent a separate office, he therefore secured boarding for himself and wife, in the Roll House, below the Bank building, corner of Maryland Street. His first desk was in the State Bank building, situated in the triangular corner, opposite the Bates House; this was kindly offered him by Mr. John H. Rea, who was clerk of the United States District Court, here he put out his shingle, and the world learnt, that Benjamin Harrison, Attorney at Law, did business at that stand. In appearance he is described as being short, of slender physique, and what might be called a blonde, with grey eyes tinged with blue, dressing plainly, and indifferent as to styles; modest in manners, with a pleasant voice and look, and possessed of a good flow of language. It may not be interesting to know that the first money he earned, was as Court Crier of the Federal Court, for which service he received during term time, the sum of two dollars and a half per day. His first professional fee, was a five dollar gold piece, paid to him at the door of his unpretentious three roomed house. During the first year of his career in Indianapolis, he had a case in which he was employed as prosecutor against a colored cook of the Roy House, whose alleged crime was putting arsenic in the hotel coffee, in revenge for some real or fancied grievance. Counsel for the defendant was Henry W. Ellsworth (son of Henry L. Ellsworth, who was for many years Commissioner of Patents), Mr. Harrison was less than half his antagionist's age, with but

a short experience at the bar, and pitted against a man of
considerable professional experience; every one thought
the result would be to his entire discomfiture, this notion
was entirely dissipated the first day of the trial, for in his usual
and quiet way, the young and comparatively unknown
lawyer, so overmatched his big and pretentious antagon-
ist, that the two seemed to have changed places. Suffice it
to say that the negro was convicted, and sent to the peni-
tentiary. From this time on his success was comparatively
rapid, and was very much strengthened by his speeches in
the first National Contest of 1856, and which may be called
his maiden effort in the political service in which he has
risen to the highest point. In 1860 he was nominated to the
position of reporter in the Supreme Court, and entered on
the duties, early in 1861, and though not a lucrative office,
still to a young lawyer whose income was small, it was a
great help. In the meantime he had changed his
boarding house from Roll's to a Mrs. Jameson's in a small
frame building, nearly opposite the Dennison House.

Whilst Mrs. Harrison was on a visit to Oxford; Russell,
her eldest child, was born on the 12th of August, 1854, and
upon returning home in the fall, the room in Mrs. Jameson's was given up, and a modest one-story house, with
three apartments, was taken; in this unpretentious abode,
the now resident of the White House, and his wife, began
their house-keeping experiences, Mrs. Harrison was
herself the house-keeper, and with the occasional aid
of "a help," assisting all she could, during all this
time Mr. Harrison fought hard against getting into debt,
and in this was successful through all this struggle for
existence, patiently, and with never a thought of com-
plaint, he worked hard for the cherished wife of his bosom,
and the dear little ones at home, possessed of ambition his ev
ery exertion was spurred on by thoughts of them. Whilst a

tenant of the little house in Vermont Street, he received
an offer to go into partnership with Mr. William Wallace,
which he accepted, and together they went into business at
Temperance Hall, on Washington Street, and remained so
until 1860, when Mr. Wallace was elected clerk of Marion
county, this caused the partnership to be dissolved, and
was succeeded by that of Fishback and Harrison, which
lasted until Mr. Harrison entered the Army in 1862, and
now appeared on the horizon of time, that cloud, no bigger
than a man's hand, that was to ultimately darken and
throw this whole country into gloom; the great slavery
question was in a state of ferment, the question between the North and South, growing out of the fact of
the latter insisting upon their right to carry slavery into
the territories, had advanced to a point of bitterness unknown in the history of the United States. Talk of war
was whispered about, and the nation at large was looking
eagerly on, watching for the first move to be taken by those
in power. When the news of the firing on Fort Sumter
was brought Mr. Harrison, he could do no more work on
that day, and like the loyal thousands of the North, his
thoughts were only of the insulted flag, and the danger of
the Union. Like many other patriotic citizens, he put
aside all personal feelings, and in July, 1862, entered the
Army, a little higher than a private, as a second lieutenant,
with a recruiting commission, raising a company of which
he was made captain. On the seventh of August he was
appointed Colonel of the 70th Indiana Regiment by Governor Morton, who being a good judge of character, thought
he saw the making of a good soldier in him.

During his first two years service, nothing of importance
occurred worthy of mention, his duties mainly consisting
of guarding bridges and commissiary stores, fighting
guerrillas, and capturing spies. As a disciplinarian he was

exceedingly strict, but many incidents of his goodness at heart might be told that occurred during his command; on long forced marches it was no unusual sight to see the Colonel walking, while some poor foot-sore private was astride of his horse. One private of the regiment, now living in Kansas, telegraphed to General Harrison on his nomination, "The congratulations of an old soldier of your regiment whose knapsack you carried when he was exhausted from sickness and fatigue."

In the Atlanta campaign he seemed to bear a charmed life, being always seen where the bullets were thickest. The battle of Resacca was a memorable engagement, the Confederates being the attacking party, during part of the fight it was a fierce struggle to see who could hold the commanding position, the Harrison regiment, and others making up the brigade pressing rapidly up toward the crest of the hill, after reaching the top they met the enemy face to face, bayonets were thrust, and muskets clubbed, at this time the Rebels captured the battery on the Union right, and immediately turned the guns on our men, so as to pour into them the most destructive infilade fire, it looked like disaster particularly as the mule trains close in the rear of the troops were filling up the road, and clogging the bridge in a way that made a stampede imminent, in the midst of all this, General Harrison was seen riding up and down, right in front of the line, waving his sword and calling on the boys to stand firm. His example held the troops, they retook the battery, and prevented what at one time, looked like complete ruin.

In the Summer of 1864, the following order was received by Colonel Harrison, of which this is a copy,

HEADQUARTERS, MILITARY DIVISION OF THE MISSISSIPPI,
IN THE FIELD, ATLANTA, GA., SEPT. 12, 1864.
SPECIAL FIELD ORDERS, } Extract.
No. 71.

III. Pursuant to instruction from the War Department,

the following officers will report in person, to Hon. O.
P. Morton, Governor of Indiana, at Indianapolis, Ind.,
for special duty. The Quarter-Master's Department
will furnish transportation. By the order of

MAJOR GENERAL W. T. SHERMAN.

L. W. DAYTON, Aid-de-Camp.

COL. BEN. HARRISON,
70th Reg't. Ind. Inf. Vol.

Immediately on his arrival at Indianapolis he reported
to Governor Morton, when he was told the nature
of the duties required of him. This was the first
opportunity of visiting his family after having been con-
tinuously in the field for two years; his special duty now
was to thoroughly canvass the State for recruits, who had
been slow to offer themselves, and upon the ninth of November, he finished the canvas.

Colonel Harrison received the rank of Brigadier-General
under a commisson signed by Abraham Lincoln, and
counter-signed by E. W. Stanton, Secretary of War, dated
March 22nd, 1865, in which it states that it was given "for,
ability and manifest energy and gallantry in command of
the brigade," and also he was to rank as such, Brevet-
Brigadier-General from the 23rd day of January, of the
year mentioned.

His certificate of discharge shows a muster out of the
service, Benjamin Harrison, Colonel and Brevet-Brigadier
70th regiment of Indiana, Infantry Volunteers; that he was
enrolled on the 7th day of August, 1862, to serve three
years or during the war, and was discharged on the 8th
day of June, 1865. at Washington, D. C. – by reason of
General Order 77 Adjutant General's office 1865 and instructions. Adjutant General's office, May 20th, 1865.

As a soldier, as in anything else General Harrison un-
dertakes, he was successful; going out without any military
training whatever, he is spoken of as becoming one of the

c'osest students of the science and art of war there was in
the army.   We have not the space in this review to give a
lengthy account of his career as a soldier, although we
might fill pages with incidents therefrom,—at New Hope
Church—at Gilgal Church—at Kenesaw—at Peach Tree
Creek, and elsewhere, did he display that wonderful pluck
that was here brought out from him and many another
man who at home were peaceable citizens.

In 1880 we find him in the National Convention at
Chicago, chairman of the delegation from Indiana, and
when many delegates insisted on using his name for the
first nomination, he positively declined.   In 1884 he again
represented his State as delegate-at-large, and he was again
discussed in connection with the nomination for the first
place on the National ticket.   The National Republican
convention at Chicago on the 19th day of June, 1889, is
still too fresh in everybody's mind, to require a detailed account; suffice it to say that the eighth and decisive ballot
showed 544 votes for General Harrison and the nomination
was of course unanimous.

The balloting for a Vice-President candidate was entered
upon immediately that order was restored and the nomi-
nators were made.   There was but one ballot; Levi P. Morton leading the list with 59 votes.—And now his honors
thick upon him Benjamin Harrison is installed in the
Presidential Chair, placed there with the confidence of the
people, and when his term of office has expired, may Republican and Democrats alike, be able to exclaim; well
done thou good and faithful servant.

The Cost of a President.

The sole income of the President of the United State from the public treasury is his salary of $50,000 a year. He draws it at the rate of $4,166⅔ a month. This is a fraction more than $960 a week, and $160 each for six working days.

Until Grant's time Presidents lived on half this salary. Experience has shown that the present sum is large enough to cover the expenses of the most extravagant households, and to leave a comfortable balance in the purse of a presidential family of moderate ideas.

Yet there is not another magistrate at the head of any people exceeding the number of 10,000,000 who does not receive a larger salary than the august, potent and toiling President of the United States.

ROYALTY COMES HIGH.

The Shah of Persia, who has nothing to do except to boss several hundred wives, is in the enjoyment of an income of $30,000,000 a year. Then there is the Czar of Russia, whose cheif duty is to keep from being blown up. He is paid something like $10,000,000 yearly. The dignified King of Siam gets along on a like sum. The royal family of poor, miserable Spain, receive $3,900,000 every year, and Italians sleep out of doors and eat nothing but macaroni to make up a purse of $3,000,000 and more for their royalties.

Such figures as these console the British peop e somewhat or their annual outlay, under specifiic laws, of $2,915,000 on Victoria and her family, to say nothing of indirect extortions and perquisits. Even now, when the Queen is parading an economical investigation of the royal pay-roll, and is turning off her master of the buckhounds, her yeomen of the guard and similar absolete guys of the opera

113

bouffe, her purpose is not to save anything for the public treasury, but to provide a fund from which she may hereafter support her grandchildren, without risking a rebuff from Parliment on the one hand or parting with her own cash on the other.

That reformed pirate of the seas, the Sultan of Morocco, is slightly compensated for his self-denial by an annual allowance of $2,500,000, and the Mikado of Japan, whom we have all seen across the footlights, receives $2,300,000. The impotent royalty of Egypt draws $1,575,000 from the substance of that tax ridden land, while the Hohenzollerns content themselves with a yearly tribute of $1,125,000 from the Prussian empire. Even the Sultan of cotton-clouted Zanzibar, pockets a million a year, and $700,000 are wrung from the Saxons of Saxony, no more considerable a community than Illinois in population or Massachusetts in geographical area, by the reighning duke and his purpled gang. Portugal, Sweden and Brazil each spend about $600,000 on their Kings.

With fewer people than live in some New York wards, and with only two-thirds of Rhode Island's area, the petty princelings of Schwarzburg Sondershausen are paid $150,000.

On the other hand, the republic of France allows her chief magistrate only $200,000, but naked little Hayti gives her presidential crowd $240,000 a year, Switzerland's Presidents comes the lowest of all the nations of the earth, his salary is $3,000 a year.

The wholly useless Governor-General of Canada receives $50,000 and so also does the Governor-General of Victoria, while the like functionary in India has a salary of $200,000.

THE PRESIDENT AND HIS HOUSEHOLD.

It appears from these quotations that, in view of the fact this is the only nation on the globe with a treasury surplus

and in view of our relative size among governments' we get
our ruling done at bottom rock price. But while not a
cent, more than $50,000 goes into the presidential pocket,
that figure does not represent the cost of the Presidency. By
far the biggest item in this expense account is the
sum spent in electing a President every four years. No
nation lavishes such a tremendous sum as we do in the suc-
cession to the chief magistracy.

A careful estimate of the total public cost yearly of the
White House, including everything from the President's
salary down, is about $150,000.

Following are the items in this estimate:

THE SALARIES.

The President	$50,000
The private secretary	3,250
The assistant secretary	2,250
Six clerks	11,200
A telegraph operator	1,400
The steward	1,800
An usher	1,460
Four messengers	4,800
Five doorkeepers	6,000
A watchman	900
The engineer	864
Total	$83,864

That is the list as it appears in the blue book. But in
addition to that there are detailed at the White House sev-
en policeman, whose salaries aggregate $7,560. This in-
creases the total to $91,224. Then the book of estimates of
the current year calls for the following allowances:

SPECIAL APPROPRIATIONS.

The President's contingent fund	$8,000 00
Care repair and furnishing the mansion	16,000 00
Gas, lamplighters, fitters, labororers, erection and repair of lightning apparatus, matches, etc.	14,000 00

Fuel 3,000 00
Repair of the water pipes and the cleaning of
    the spring 800 00
Care and repair of the greenhouses 5,000 00
Improvement and maintenance of the grounds .   6,500 00
Erecting and maintaining electric lights 2,788 50
A watchman 660 00

    Total allowances $56,748 50
Salary list 91,424 00

    Grand total $148,172 50

In addition to these already enumerated are four waiters
and pantrymen, a marketman, an assistant cook, a house-
keeper, a lamplighter, a fireman, two laundry-women, a
gardener and about a dozen assistants, two stablemen and
a driver. This makes the total number of people employed
at public expense, at the White House, 57. But I believe
the specific appropriations and the allowances which I
have quoted cover about the entire public expense of the
presidential establishment. The President pays the chief
cook, who resides over the kitchen during the social season,
out of his private funds.

The Government aims to provide the President with
everything, from his matches to his silver service, except-
ting only the important item of food.

The people would submit to a good deal larger expendi-
ture at the executive mansion. They seem to want something glittering and impressive there.

(Boston Globe.)

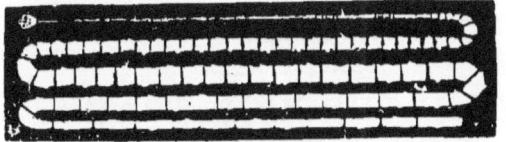